SHOOT TO KILL

As Spur turned the bay mare and moved toward the barn, he saw a glint of metal to the left behind a pair of pine trees. Automatically he grabbed the rifle out of the boot and dove off the bay.

Just as he dove he felt a bullet whip through the air where his head had been a fraction of a second before. The sound of the shot came almost on top of the bullet and with it came another pair of shots, and Spur figured there was a gunman amid the pine trees and another in the barn.

The gun from the trees blasted again twice, and this time one round came close enough to make Spur gasp. He screamed as if in sudden pain and then let the screams grow weaker and weaker until they faded out. He drew his six-gun, held it by his side and waited....

Also in the *Spur* Series by *Leisure Books:*

SPUR

38

FREE PRESS FILLY

DIRK FLETCHER

LEISURE BOOKS   NEW YORK CITY

A LEISURE BOOK®

February 1993

Published by

Dorchester Publishing Co., Inc.
276 Fifth Avenue
New York, NY 10001

The name ''Leisure Books'' and the stylized ''L'' with design are trademarks of Dorchester Publishing Co., Inc.

Printed in the United States of America.

Chapter One

Andrew Weston Pinnick stood outside his office and bellowed at a pair of ruffians who had just shot two holes in the door of the *Clarion* newspaper building.

"Be off, you scallywags. You don't scare me none. I eat your kind for breakfast and belch garlic all afternoon. Be gone. Go tell your boss he doesn't scare me either. Nobody on God's green earth is going to stop me from printing the truth and from expressing my opinions about the way this town and county are run. Just a damn shame more people in this county don't stand up to them bastards."

He whirled and marched back into his office. The front window remained boarded up after it had been shot out four times in two months. A small fire had singed the back storage room, but luckily he quickly had put it out. He even had time to take a shot at the two yahoos who must have started the fire.

He knew he was hurting them, exposing to the public what they were doing. They had vandalized his type cases two weeks ago when he had lost two days as he and Gypsy got the mixed-up fonts and sizes and letters all back in the right print trays. He didn't even think how many thousands of individual letters there were in each tray. That day he had wanted to quit—but he didn't.

He wouldn't stop exposing them until they killed him, but he gambled that they wouldn't go that far. They were not that secure, that strong yet. But if their gigantic swindle went through, they just might be strong enough to have him killed.

He had to prevent that swindle and protect the damned public and the Territory of Arizona, even if they didn't seem to know what he was doing— or maybe didn't care. Since Wednesday was press day, the louts always came after him then. So far they hadn't hurt either him or Gypsy. If they touched his daughter he'd forget himself, take his shotgun and start killing them. He would take any abuse they could throw at him, but he wouldn't allow even a scratch on his perfect, gracious, lovely daughter. He had sworn that promise to his Lilly as she lay on her death bed three years ago.

"Hey, sourpuss," Gypsy said. "Smile, Papa, we ain't beaten yet. I have just one more column to proofread and correct, and we'll be ready to print the first page. I like that front page editorial. I set it in ten point bold like you said, and it looks fine.

"That's going to cause a lot of comment. Should get some reaction from the territorial capital, if anything will."

Gypsy Pinnick smiled at her father. She was 19, slender and shapely like her mother had been, with sleek black hair that hung like a dark river to well below her waist.

Gypsy had a rosebud mouth, even white teeth, a great smile, and cheek bones so high they almost touched her eyes. He smile dazzled, and right now she stepped over to her father and rubbed the back of his neck and his shoulders.

"You're tense again. Why don't you have a nap? You'll need it before we get tonight's last page printed."

"Work to do."

"Nonsense, your work is coming tonight. I'll clean up this last column, make the corrections and pull one more proof for you to double-check. Now stretch out on that cot in back and relax for a while even if you can't sleep."

Andrew Pinnick stretched. Three or four places in his body didn't hurt him at all today. That was progress. "Maybe just for ten minutes. Anybody comes bothering, you blow that whistle like I showed you."

Gypsy's face broke into a grin, and she nodded. "Right, Papa, and I've got that .22 pistol in my desk drawer. Now get out of here."

He tried to get one more look at the front page proof, but his daughter covered it up and shooed him toward the back room.

Gypsy watched him go, then settled down to proofreading the last story on the front page, about a logger who had been killed when a tree he cut down ricocheted on its many large limbs and shot back at him ten feet beyond the stump.

She found two mistakes and marked them, then took the sheet to the composing table where she selected the correct letters from the type tray.

It took her 15 minutes to locate all the errors and correct them. Then she tightened the type in the heavy form and tapped it all down with a wooden mallet and a leather-covered block of wood to be sure all the letters were level. That done, she put the heavy page on the small proof press and inked the top thoroughly with a rubber roller.

Gypsy placed a sheet of proof paper over the form and pulled the heavy roller over the page, transferring the ink onto the paper.

When the roller stopped at the end, she peeled the page away from the type and studied it. Yes, the corrections were in place. She would let her father take one more look at it, but by then it would be too late to make any more changes.

Gypsy marveled at how her father had stood up to the richest man in town, J. Lawton Benscoter, who owned the six biggest stores in town and controlled the county politics with a choking grip. During the past five years the tension between the two men had increased to the point where they never spoke to each other except at Pine Grove Town Council meetings and other official functions.

Gypsy wondered if J. Lawton was behind the violence aimed at the newspaper over the past six months. She wasn't sure but he was certainly one candidate.

She saw that her father had fallen asleep. Good, he needed it. It was late Wednesday afternoon, and they would be working until midnight to get everything printed. There were 340 papers to print this week, a few more than last week. She tried to get more into circulation each time so they could at least pretend they were making progress.

As it was, they were barely scraping by. Advertising was what they needed, and with so few stores in town . . . She frowned. No, there were enough stores in Pine Grove to produce at least six pages a week. That is, there would be if the six largest stores in town would advertise but they didn't since they were all owned by J. Lawton Benscoter, who ran the whole town. Her father and Benscoter had been fighting for two years now about everything.

Her father was right, and Mr. Benscoter was plain stubborn. Gypsy shook her head, not understanding the whole thing, and went to wake up her father. They had to start printing or they'd be there all night.

An hour later, they had the first two pages finished. Running their old press was twice the work it would be if they had a newer one, but that was out of the question.

As she did every Wednesday night about six o'clock, Gypsy went across the street to the Home Café. Terri would have their dinners all ready to take out. His specialty Wednesday was beef stew, and he put up two bowls along with bread and coffee and all the trimmings. He had it in a cardboard box, ready and waiting.

Gypsy stopped to talk a minute. She'd known Terri for over three years now, ever since he opened the café.

"How many pages this week, big newspaper writer?" Terri asked, a twinkle in his eye.

"Six, but it should have been four. I wish you could afford to advertise. We'll almost break even this week."

They talked for five minutes, then Gypsy realized the stew was getting cold. She paid Terri, thanked him and went out the front door.

"Fire!" somebody down the block yelled. Gypsy looked down the street and saw ugly black smoke rising over some stores across the way.

Three stores were attached, wall to wall, then after an empty lot was her father's building. She ran down the boardwalk and soon saw smoke pouring from the front of the *Clarion* building.

Gypsy dropped the box of supper, raced across the street and stopped in front of the building. Flames roared out the door and through the cracks between the boards where the windows had been.

A man looked in the door, then darted back, choking from the smoke.

"My father's still in there!" Gypsy screamed and lunged toward the door. Strong hands caught her and stopped her.

"Try around back," somebody shouted.

A bucket brigade raced up, drawing water from the pump at the horse trough. The lead man threw the half-filled buckets of water through the front door, but it had little effect on the fire.

A man came around from the rear of the building, shaking his head. "Not a chance. Back door is one mass of flames. Looks like the fire started back there."

"Do something!" Gypsy screamed. "Do something to help my father."

Terri came up beside her, put his arm around her and held her tightly.

"Gypsy, they're trying. Looks like the fire had a big head start. Them buckets of water ain't gonna put out the fire. Maybe your pa got out the back door."

Terri turned to the crowd that had gathered. "Has anyone seen Mr. Pinnick, the newspaper man?" he yelled. Nobody answered, but Gypsy saw some heads shake.

Mrs. Natterson, a widow who ran the Ladies Wear shop three doors down, hurried up and put her arm around Gypsy.

"Dear girl, I know your pa is safe somewhere. A body doesn't stay inside a building like that when it's burning up. He's here somewhere, you can bet on it."

Mrs. Natterson led Gypsy away from the heat of the flames. Now the bucket brigade threw its water on the building 40 feet away to keep it from catching.

Gypsy could hear Terri calling through the crowd, asking if anyone had seen Mr. Pinnick. Slowly the truth came to her. Someone had set fire at the front door and at the back door at the same moment. This time the people trying to silence the paper had done it. They had counted on trapping her father inside and had waited until she went for their supper.

It had become an established pattern. Most folks in town knew they worked Wednesday night printing the paper. After watching for two weeks, anyone would know about when she went to the café to bring back their supper.

They had torched the building from both ends on purpose. They wanted to kill the paper and at the same time kill her father.

J. Lawton Benscoter had to be the one. He was the only man in town rich enough and powerful enough to hire men to do something like this. The

two arsonists were probably on their horses and
five miles out of town by now with their blood
money in their pockets.

J. Lawton Benscoter! She would bring him
down if it was the last thing she did. But how?

Mrs. Natterson turned and looked Gypsy in the
eye.

"I can't keep up hope for you, Gypsy. We've
looked everywhere. Nobody has seen your father
since the fire started. There's a chance he was
inside and couldn't get out."

Gypsy nodded. "I know, Mrs. Natterson. J.
Lawton Benscoter hired someone to burn down
the *Clarion*. He told them to torch both the front
door and the back. He deliberately murdered my
father, and I intend to make him pay."

Mrs. Benscoter frowned. "Gypsy, I understand
your anguish, but don't just jump to conclu-
sions. Lots of things could have happened. A
can of paint could have exploded, and your Pa
could have been knocked unconscious. Something might have fallen on him. Don't go putting
any blame, leastwise until it can be proved. I
know your Pa and Benscoter didn't get on too
well."

They walked to the back of the shell of the building. The roof caved in, showering the darkening
sky with a million sparks. Soon there were only a
few timbers left where the 50 foot-long building
had stood.

Gypsy watched it and shook her head.

"Everything is ruined, lost, burned up. All of
the equipment and the type destroyed. I have
to start over. We don't have much money in the
bank, but I have my dowry. Pa was old fashioned
about that."

"You come home with me for tonight, Gypsy," Mrs. Natterson said. "Things will look a little better in the morning. I know you've lost a lot tonight, but something will turn up tomorrow."

"No, Mrs. Natterson, nothing will be different tomorrow. I've got to do myself whatever needs to be done, and I'm going to start tonight. Do you have some paper and envelopes? I want to write some letters. I wrote a news article once telling people they had to take matters into their own hands sometimes. If the territorial officials were crooked, they had to write to the territorial attorney general and tell him. Write to the governor or a United States senator or even the president. Tell everybody what's wrong, and you stand a good chance that somebody will do something about it.

"That's what I'm going to do tonight, start writing letters. This is a blow against freedom of the press. It's in the constitution, in the bill of rights. I'll write to the *New York* Times and tell them what happened here. They'll listen. Somebody will listen. Somebody has to listen."

Gypsy sagged against Mrs. Natterson and only then did the tears come. She cried it all out in the next two hours. Mrs. Natterson took her home, fixed her a bath and then settled her down in a featherbed.

Ten minutes later, Gypsy was up asking for pen, paper and envelopes. That night she wrote ten letters to everyone she could think of who might help.

The first one went to the President of the United States, then to two senators, then the Justice Department. After that she wrote to three national newspapers. Next came the territorial officials right there in Arizona.

*   *   *

The next morning at daylight, Gypsy walked through the cooling ashes of the *Clarion* building. She would rebuild in the same spot and that meant saving what equipment she could. The case of type had not been tipped over during the fire, and only the font on the top had been harmed. Most of it was half-melted together. The rest of the cases of type were in good shape so, she had a start. Even the proof press could be salvaged. An hour later Sheriff Ben Willard came. He held his hat in his hand as he spoke to her.

"Miss Pinnick, I'm sorry about the fire. Best if you stand aside so we can search to see if your pa really was inside here last night."

She walked down to Terri's cafe and waited. A half hour later a soot-blackened Sheriff Willard came to see her. He was a medium-sized man with pot belly and a pinched face.

"Miss Pinnick, I'm sorry to report that we did find your father's remains. He must have crawled under the heavy metal of the press. The smoke and fumes probably caused his death since he ain't burned any. We took him down to the undertaker."

Gypsy thanked him and went to say good-bye to her father.

The funeral was that afternoon with half the people in town attending at the Methodist church. When it was over Gypsy went directly to the bank.

Mr. Gleason told her the newspaper account, which she now controlled, had a balance of $67.53. Her own dowry account had an even $1,000 plus interest coming up for the quarter.

When she got back to the *Clarion* shell, she saw Terri waiting for her. Nearby were 20 men with shovels, saws, hammers and other tools.

"Figured we could get a start on raising an office for you, Gypsy," Terri said. "Hear you want to rebuild. First we'll put up a tent to store what you can save. Then we figure to load up and haul off all the trash and burned timbers and such."

A tear squeezed out of Gypsy Pinnick's eye and worked slowly down her cheek. When she reached up and kissed Terri on the cheek, somebody in the crowd cheered.

She turned and smiled at them.

"Thank you, everyone. Now, let's get to work!"

Chapter Two

Spur McCoy had finished a case in Los Angeles and wired his boss in Washington D.C. for instructions. Should he return to his home base in St. Louis, or was there another problem on the coast he should look into while he was there?

The return wire came before he had finished his lunch. He opened the yellow envelope and read:

"TO: SPUR MCCOY, COAST HOTEL, LOS ANGELES, CALIFORNIA. LEAVE AT ONCE FOR ARIZONA. SMALL TOWN OF PINE GROVE SOUTH OF FLAGSTAFF ABOUT 30 MILES. POSSIBLE (VIOLATION OF FREEDOM OF THE PRESS AND) MURDER OF NEWSPAPER'S EDITOR/PUBLISHER. CONTACT GYPSY PINNICK. REPORT EXTENT OF CASE AND YOUR PROGRESS. EXPENSE

FUNDS WIRED TODAY. GENERAL WILTON D. HALLECK SENDING."

An hour later, Spur McCoy sat on a southbound train, heading for San Diego. From there he would take another train to Phoenix and, that was as far as the rail lines had been laid. To get further north, he'd take a stagecoach to Pine Grove. Freedom of the press was always a touchy problem. Often it was a clash between a young, poor newspaperman and a wealthy, older businessman involved in some kind of skullduggery. Money and power often had its own way in spite of a crusading newspaperman, often with tragic results.

He read the wire again. Gypsy Pinnick? Could be either a man or a woman, widow or son or daughter of the dead man. He'd find out. He had nearly two hours before he changed trains in San Diego.

McCoy pulled his black flat-brimmed hat down over his eyes and relaxed. He was a Secret Service agent, one of the few federal lawmen who had jurisdiction in all of the states and territories. From his office in St. Louis, he prowled the western half of the nation at the bidding of General Halleck in Washington D.C.

The agency had been started by President Lincoln specifically to protect the currency. In the years since then, the Secret Service had taken on many other duties, including the protection of the president himself. William Wood was director of the Secret Service, having been appointed by the president. He then selected a small group of agents to work directly for the federal government in any aspect of law enforcement where federal regulations had been violated or local law authorities had asked for help.

McCoy was in his thirties, with dark hair and intense green eyes. He stood just shy of six-two and weighed 195 pounds. He had graduated from Harvard University in Boston, served in the Civil War reaching the rank of captain, and joined the Secret Service not long after it was organized.

McCoy's father owned several large retail and import companies in New York, but McCoy had decided he didn't want to follow in his father's footsteps in the business world. Since he could shoot and ride better than any other Secret Service agent, he was assigned to the western section of the nation.

McCoy felt someone sit down beside him, but he left his hat over his eyes.

"I beg your pardon?"

The voice was female and youthful. He took a chance, raised the brim of his hat and looked into a pair of soft blue eyes surrounded by a pretty face and billows of long, curly blonde hair. He pushed back his hat and nodded.

"You were speaking to me?"

"You're the only person in this seat and I'm looking directly at you, so I'd have to at least suppose that I must be talking to you."

"So?"

"I was wondering if you knew when we get to San Diego."

"Scheduled for two-forty-six this afternoon. That should be not quite two hours yet."

"Oh!" Her pretty face clouded. "That doesn't leave much time."

McCoy grinned. "Depends on time to do what. If you need time to breathe, we have plenty. Time for a short nap, the same. Time to write a symphony or build a bridge over a great body of water would be a little short."

"True." She looked away, then bit her lip and stared back at him. "It was a childish, stupid thing to do."

McCoy enjoyed watching this pretty girl. He figured she was not much over 18, dressed well, no rings on her left hand.

"Just what was this stupid thing you did?" he asked.

"I made a bet with Madelyn, my former best friend over there on the other side of the train."

"Former best friend. That sounds serious."

"Serious for me, probably not for you. You see the bet I made with Madelyn was—"

The girl stopped, closed her eyes and sighed. Her mouth set in a firm line, and her chin came up a little.

"I bet Madelyn that I could get you to kiss me on the lips before we got to San Diego."

McCoy laughed softly. "You make bets like that often?"

"First one ever. We saw you get on, and one word led to another, and we both remarked what a . . . what a great body you had. Then I impulsively made the bet. Do you hate me?"

McCoy chuckled and looked at her. She sat tall in the seat, slender, well-formed, a long white neck and now defiant blue eyes.

"No, I don't hate you. What did you bet for?"

"I can't say."

McCoy tilted up her head by touching under her chin. He looked over at Madelyn who stared at them. McCoy reached down and kissed the blonde on the lips, came away, then when he saw her eyes still closed, he kissed her again, harder this time and brushing his tongue against her lips.

Her face blossomed into a beautiful smile, and she nodded.

"Thanks, maybe I'll see you in San Diego."

"I'm going on through to Phoenix."

He saw the relief in her eyes. "Now, if you don't mind, I want to continue the nap you interrupted."

"Yes. I get to go collect on my bet. Thanks." She hesitated, then sat on the edge of the seat.

"Why did you kiss me?"

"Why? You're a beautiful lady and spunky enough to do what you did. I like women like that. Of course, you do have quite a bit more growing up to do."

"I know, but it's going to be fun." She touched his shoulder, stood and scurried across the aisle and up one seat to Madelyn, the look of astonished surprise still on the losing girl's face.

McCoy settled back, brought his hat down over his eyes and caught a small nap to the click-click of the steel wheels going over the track sections every 30 feet.

Much later, he made his change of trains in San Diego, had to wait three hours to get moving again and arrived in Phoenix sometime during the night.

McCoy felt the heat of the day still contained in the vaulted ceiling of the railroad station. Phoenix was a firebox in the summer, and this was summer.

He caught the stage that left at six A.M. and arrived in Pine Grove, after three delays, at a little before four in the afternoon. At once he checked into the Pine Grove Hotel, ordered bath water and tried to become halfway human again. McCoy didn't hate to travel; it was that it simply took up so much time and sapped his energy.

After a solid meal in the Home Café, he looked up Gypsy Pinnick.

He knocked on a modest house a block from Main Street and two blocks down from the center of town. Moments later a curious young woman stared at him through a screen door that appeared to be locked.

"Miss Pinnick?"

"Yes."

"I'm Spur McCoy, United States Secret Service agent. I've come in response to your several letters about what happened to your father and your newspaper here."

Gypsy let out a small cry of wonder, unlocked the screen door and opened it. "Thank the Lord! Won't you come in. I've been praying that somebody would come and help us. So far we don't have any clues as to who might have set the fire. We found kerosene cans at both doors of the building where the *Clarion* was published, but we can't prove who used it to start the deadly blaze."

She led him into the small house, offered him a seat on the couch and curled into a chair nearby. "Oh, could I offer you some coffee or tea?"

"I just ate, thank you. Could I ask you to show me the site of the fire before it gets dark?"

"Good idea," Gypsy said. "I should have thought of that." Her smile made the task of trying to find the cold trail of an arsonist a little more interesting.

They poked through what was left of the rubble of the building. Most of the smaller debris had been carted off. A tent with a plank floor contained what had been salvaged from the fire.

"Not much we can use," Gypsy said. "We got the proof press working, so I turned out an extra edition a week ago. Just two pages and the same size as the letterhead paper we found in the rubble. I made only a hundred copies, but posted them around town. I offered a reward for anyone finding my father's killer. I made it a regular edition, just smaller. Don't want to break the paper's reputation of publishing every week since Papa founded it back fourteen years ago."

"Most of the type came through?"

"Almost all but the top case, some circus wood type, two inches tall. We seldom used it anyway except in a few ads."

"All of your back issues must have been lost."

"Not true, Mr. McCoy. I made sure of that. After the first small fire we had, I took a complete historical file of our fourteen years of issues home and put them in a steamer trunk. They're all safe and sound.

"Good, I'll want to look over those for the past two years. I want to know exactly who your father was fighting and why. It all should be in the papers."

"Should be, but isn't. I can tell you right now he had a running fight with the town's richest man, J. Lawton Benscoter. He's got enough money to hire men to burn down our building and then get out of town so fast they'll never be found."

"One suspect. Who else did your father pick a fight with?"

Gypsy wrinkled her forehead as she thought. The slight frown even looked attractive on her.

"I guess he didn't have any other real enemies. Oh, he took shots at anyone who he thought stepped out of line on the town council or in the legislature. He told me once he thought something really big was brewing, but evidently it simmered down. He never mentioned it again, and he certainly didn't write any big banner headlines about it or do an editorial. Papa liked to do hard-driving editorials. He shamed the town council into starting our public library and also rode them so hard they decided to buy one of those new pumper fire engines, just as soon as they get enough money. I'm not sure how they work, but they throw a stream of water from a hose. Bet that new fire engine pumper would have saved our building."

"Pine Grove is the county seat of Pine County, right?" Spur asked.

Gypsy nodded.

"Means you have a county sheriff in town. How did your father get along with the lawman?"

"Not real well. Pa was critical of him at times. Pa said that Sheriff Ben Willard was about as much good as an udder on a bull." She laughed to cover up her embarrassment.

"He go after the sheriff in print lately?"

"Not that I remember. He did write an editorial for the front page about the sale of some timber rights just outside of town for what Pa called a scandalously low price."

"Who bought the timber rights?" Spur asked.

"Oh, a man here in town we call Loophole Larson. He's a lawyer, one of only three in town and the best one. He claims he can find a loophole for his client in any lawsuit or any contract or bill of sale that was ever written. Usually he does."

"What does a lawyer want with timber rights?"

"Pa said it was to sell the rights to a third party who did not want to bid publicly on them."

"Nothing illegal about that. Is there a sawmill in town or nearby?"

"That's what Pa said was strange. There isn't a sawmill here. One up at Flagstaff, but that's thirty-two miles due north of us. Pa said wouldn't be economically feasible to haul the logs up there to saw them."

"I agree. Any talk of the railroad coming up this way from Phoenix?"

"A little talk, but no action. Nothing up here the rails can help. Some timber, but not enough to pay for it. Don't figure us or Flag will ever get railroad service."

"Bet there are a bunch of teamsters who are happy about that," Spur said.

"Deed they are. A young teamster came sparking me for a time, but he left town to work out of Phoenix. Said there was more work down there. I wasn't about to leave Pa and the paper. Anyway he never down-on-his-knee proposed to me."

"The young man was a fool," Spur said.

"Mr. McCoy, you shouldn't be talking that way." She grinned. "I do like to hear it, but right now we got to concentrate on Pa and who set those fires and who paid them."

The afternoon turned to dusk.

"Miss Pinnick, I have a room at the hotel, but I would like to bother you for a few minutes first to look over some of the past few issues of your paper. There may be something in there to give me a hint about what your father was fighting."

"That's easy. I might even boil us a pot of coffee to go with the cinnamon rolls I made this morning."

It was nearly nine that evening when Spur turned the last page of the weekly newspaper and put it back on the stack. The coffee and cinnamon rolls were all gone. He had four issues to go. He had checked every story for the past two months.

"That's enough for me tonight, Miss Pinnick. I've had a long day. I'll come tomorrow morning and check these last four issues if it's all right."

"Yes, of course—and please call me Gypsy. Everyone in town does."

He said he would, told her to call him Spur and headed down toward Main and the Pine Grove Hotel. Spur made it a habit of keeping his hotel key in his pocket, not advertising to one and all that he was not in his room when his key was in the box. He walked past the room clerk's desk and looked at the spot labeled room 212. No messages.

He hurried up to his second floor room and inserted the key into the simple door lock. He turned the handle and, keeping behind the wall, pushed the door in hard so it would swing all the way to the wall.

It did and made a klunking sound when the knob hit the wall. No one behind the door. He edged around the doorjamb and peered into the room, dimly lighted by the hallway coal oil lamp. He saw no one.

Spur stepped into the room, struck a match, flamed the coal oil lamp, turned up the wick and put the glass chimney back in place.

Something moved in the far corner of the room, and before he could reach for his colt .45, a woman walked out of the shadows toward him.

"Spur McCoy, I've got a present for you—me." She was pretty, red-headed, beautifully sculptured—and naked.

Chapter Three

The naked girl who smiled at Spur McCoy looked a bit shopworn around the edges, but she was there and she was willing. Even as his eyes feasted on her delicious body, he wondered what kind of a price or consequence went along with the obvious delights.

She walked up to him, making everything move and wiggle and bounce. Even her modest breasts did an enticing dance.

"Naked Flo is here to make you feel good. I specialize in relieving tensions and making swellings go down. Does that get your blood boiling?"

"Might. Depends why you're here, who sent you and who paid you."

Flo turned away from him. "The very idea! Nobody paid me and nobody sent me. I saw you come in a couple of hours ago and knew I had to get a good poking from you or I couldn't sleep tonight. I'm not a whore, if that's what you're thinking."

"Just a part-time paid pussy, I understand. Now who sent you up here?"

She turned and watched him, but he could read nothing in her angry stare. Then her face softened as the anger faded.

"Nobody. I sleep only with those I want to, and nobody orders me around. If you're not interested in a wild night in bed, we'll just forget it."

"You'll put your clothes on and go home to your husband."

"I didn't say that, but I am married. He's not what you'd call a responsive man. Sometimes I like to get a little sexy with a stranger. Anything wrong with that?"

"Probably. I'm no expert on deviant personalities, but I had a professor who was." As Spur watched her naked form he couldn't hold back the erection that was building at his crotch. She was long and lean, flat-bellied, with slender thighs and delicious legs. Her breasts were still slightly upthrust with youth, and he guessed she was no more than 22 or 23. She might talk more in bed with him and let something slip if she was working for somebody. It might be worth a try.

He motioned her over to the bed and sat down. She slid down beside him, her thigh touching his.

"Let's talk about this in a friendly way. Any objections?"

She shook her head and leaned toward him, and when he didn't move away, she reached up and kissed his lips. Her tongue darted between his lips and into his mouth.

"Sometimes I feel so damn sexy I don't know what to do," she said when the steamy kiss ended. Her arms went around his neck, and she pulled him into another kiss. When she broke it off, her breath came faster.

"Pine Grove is a small town, so it's hard to have an affair that everyone in the county doesn't know about. But a traveling man in the hotel is another matter. No one to watch, no one checking our house, and the man is here today and tonight, makes his calls tomorrow and takes the afternoon stage for Flagstaff."

She placed one hand on his crotch and felt his erection. Her eyes glistened and a smile enlivened her face.

"So you do like me. Good. Let's get you out of your pants. Hell, I don't care about making you naked. I just want to get to your cock and play with him."

"What's your name?" Spur asked.

"Flo, Florence. I'm Florence Benscoter, Mrs. Florence Benscoter. Now, that's enough. You'll be leaving on the train tomorrow?"

"We can talk about that later." From what Gypsy had told him Benscoter was a middle-aged man in his fifties. This girl wasn't 25 yet. Was she J. Lawton's wife? She caught him around the neck and fell backwards, pulling him with her flat on the bed.

He lay on top of her and gave a little yelp of delight.

She rolled them over so she was on top and pounded her hips against his hips three times. "Just a sample. I've got the wildest ass in town." She slid off him and undid his belt buckle, then his gunbelt buckle and worked on the buttons at his fly. He started to help, but she kissed his hands away.

"Hey, make me earn it. I want your prick so bad that I'll tear these fucking buttons off if I have to." She looked up with a little girl face to spice the sexy talk.

With the buttons open, she stood and pulled off his boots, then snaked down his pants and stripped them off him. She hung the gunbelt on the head of the bed and smiled down at him.

"Oh, yes, that's how I like to see a man, laying on his back with his big cock just making a tent out of his underwear."

Spur wore some of the new, short, cotton underwear, and she pulled them down until his erection popped into sight.

"My gawd!" she yelped. "This must be heaven!" She knelt on the bed and kissed his purple-headed shaft. "My gawd but he's gorgeous, and he's all mine for all night."

Her kisses flowed down from the point along the shaft to his pubic hair. Her fingers toyed gently with his scrotum and the heavy balls inside.

"My gawd, what a man! How come no woman hog-tied you and kept you in her bedroom? You don't wear a wedding band."

"Still looking for the right woman," he said. It was his standard reply and came with no thought on his part.

"Benscoter. Didn't I see a sign with that name, Benscoter Merchandiser and General Store?"

"You did. I'm married to J. Lawton Benscoter, richest damn man in town. Yes, he's old enough to be my father. No, he don't fuck worth a shit. Yes, he still tries, but I need some poking more than once a fucking month." She sighed. "There now, I've told you all about me and my miseries. You want a good poking, or are you all talk?"

Spur pulled her down on top of him and moved her higher until he could drop one of her breasts into his mouth. He chewed a while, nibbling at her already erect nipple, then moved to the other orb. As he worked on that one he felt her blood pressure soar and her breathing quicken.

He reached one hand between her legs, found her hard clit and twanged it four times.

Flo exploded into a grunting, wailing climax that made her pound her hips against his a dozen times. Then the spasms hit her, and she shook and trembled and vibrated until he thought she'd shake herself into pieces.

"Oh, gawd! Oh, gawd! Oh, gawd!" she whispered. Then a long wailing moan came from her mouth and the vibrations tailed off. Then before she got a good breath a new set of spasms hit her, and she pounded her hips against him again and shuddered through three more climaxes before she trembled one last time and let out a long sigh of wonder.

Her eyes opened slowly. "Gawd damn! I almost never cum that way before I get poked once or twice. Gawd damn, but you are a sexy smooth one. What the fuck is it gonna be like once you get into my little pussy and start whanging away at me?"

"Better, I hope," Spur said. He was holding back with a lot of effort. Now he rolled her off him, spread her legs and slid between them. He lifted her knees and pushed them apart.

"Hurry, you big fucker, hurry. I can't keep this up all night. I want your prick inside me right now."

He bent, probed a moment, then daggered home into her wonderland. Flo's eyes went wide, then she gasped and shrilled a long high wail as he penetrated to the roots of his sword.

"Oh, damn!" Flo said with an expression of rapture and wonder. "Now . . . this . . . is . . . what . . . it always damn should be."

Spur knew there would be more than one fuck, so he wanted this one for himself. He pulled up his knees, thrust the deepest he could, and then pounded forward, pistoning into her as fast and hard as he could.

She wailed and humped back at him but couldn't match his speed. At that rate it wouldn't take him long, Spur knew, and he panted and gasped, then roared as he plunged into her, planting his load.

When he finally relaxed and sagged against her, he felt her arms pin him in place so she could enjoy the afterglow longer.

When she at last let go, she pushed him off her and turned on her side so she could see him. Tears brimmed in her eyes.

"I never cry after making love. Almost never. Why are you so damn good and my husband so damn bad in bed? Why am I so lucky? Sure, I married the richest man in town, but what the hell has that to do with making it a good marriage? He don't want no kids. Says they just get in the way. Says he had two already by his first wife and they are nothing but trouble. He waits until I bleed and gets me then so I can't have a kid. He's terrible."

Spur kept quiet. He had nothing to offer. Advice was the last thing she wanted. At first he figured she was a tempting bit of fluff sent by someone to find out who he was and why he was here. He decided that someone controlled this town right down to the bedrooms.

Looked like Flo was on the other side, but she didn't know it. He figured if what she said had any truth in it at all, she was in no way trying to pump him for information. She probably didn't even go through his luggage.

She reached over and kissed his forehead with a feather touch. "Oh, gawd, but that was fine. You know while you were getting it off, I had three more orgasms. Three more! Damn but you are a wonder."

Flo watched him a moment. "I didn't see no sample cases. Maybe you ain't a drummer, after all. You gonna be in town for long?"

"Not sure, Flo. I'm not a drummer. Sorry."

"Oh, no, I'm glad. Maybe you'll be here a week, and I can get good poking like this every night. That would be pure heaven to me, Spur McCoy. Oh, I checked the register downstairs. The night clerk and I have a little arrangement going. He lets me know when a great stud comes into the hotel. For that he gets his way with me once a month. He's not a good lover, but I'm training him. He's only twenty-one and has more energy and sperm than he can use."

They both sat up.

"Now I've offended you. Gawd damn. Didn't want to do that. I can get us a late supper sent up from the kitchen if you want. You hungry? Young men get hungry after a fine poking, but old men get sleepy. Damn, you don't look sleepy to me."

Spur laughed. "You are some woman, Flo Benscoter. No late supper. Give me ten minutes and we'll see what else we can cook up between us that's good to eat."

Her eyes widened and she grinned. "I'm getting hungry already."

As he sat there, Spur wondered if there was some way he could utilize this windfall. Would Flo know anything about her husband's dealings? Would she know about any big operation he was working on, something big enough to kill a newspaper publisher to keep it quiet? He would try to find out, but it might take several nights like this. Spur grinned. Somehow he'd have to bear up under the rugged working conditions.

Sometime around three in the morning they came up for air, and he probed gently about her husband.

"Your man, he's a big gun in this town, I'd guess?"

"Yeah, thinks he is. Wants to be governor he says. Big deal."

"How can a man in a town this size ever be territorial governor?"

"Oh, J. Lawton has all sorts of big plans. Says he's working on a deal right now that will shake up the whole damn territory. That's J. Lawton—big talker, quick fucker."

It was a bite, a start. At last they got to sleep about four in the morning, and Spur didn't wake up until nearly seven. That was late for him. He slid out of bed before she woke up and shaved and dressed. He wasn't ready for any morning pokings.

He had a big day ahead—more research on the back issues. He wondered how to handle this case. Maybe he should get a job with Benscoter and work it from the inside. No, that wouldn't work. Benscoter would be suspicious. Spur knew people had seen him at the paper's burned-out building and going into Gypsy's house. Even the walls have eyes in a small town like this.

Flo woke up and grinned. "Now that was a night to remember. Can I come back tonight?"

"What will J. Lawton think?

"He's used to it. He knows I fuck around."

"We'll see about tonight later. I've got some work to do today first. Got to earn my pay or I'll get fired."

"What work?"

"I'm with some people who buy property and then develop it and sell it again. Not sure what's in town worth considering, but that's my job. Oh, don't tell Benscoter. He'd jack the price up on anything we wanted."

"Last thing I'd do," she said.

"Good." He hesitated. "You going to get dressed and come have breakfast?"

"Yes, but at a different restaurant. The prying eyes of a small town, you know."

He had breakfast at the Home Café, then caught Gypsy at her place just before she left for the office. She picked out the four issues he hadn't read and took them along.

"I figure you can read them at the office—my tent, that is—and then ask me any questions."

As they walked along, he tried to figure out what could be of tremendous value around this section of the country. They were in the mountains. The San Francisco mountains were north of Flagstaff and the Mazatzal mountains to the south. The Mogollon rim and its plateau lay to the east.

The village of Pine Grove lay in a small pocket with an elevation of 7,419 feet, one of the highest towns in Arizona. You can't buy and sell mountains. Maybe there were some mineral deposits, but so far nothing much had been discovered. There wasn't much so far for anyone to get worked up enough about to kill a newspaper publisher. Spur hoped that there was a story somewhere in the last few issues of the *Clarion* that would give him a lead—some hint, some smell was all he hoped for.

It had to be something that the general public didn't know about yet. What else was there? Grazing rights maybe, a railroad coming through which always made a lucky few rich, but there didn't seem to be any reason to bring in the rails. No coal, no minerals, nothing the railroad could make money on hauling back out.

As they walked to the newspaper, Spur compared Gypsy Pinnick with the woman he just spent the night with. Gypsy was much prettier and younger, just as sleekly built and with what he guessed were much larger breasts. It was a winning combination.

"Oh, I got a letter yesterday from a man in Phoenix. He's a pressman, says he's rebuilt burned-out presses before. I hired him to come up and see what we need to get the press running and to tell me how much it will cost for parts. Most of it's metal. I can't see how it was hurt much, but right now it won't work."

"Can you afford it?"

She sighed. "For a few months. I have some money, not a lot, but if I can get the paper going again I'll get some advertising and the legal ads the county has to run. Oh, it makes me so mad that J. Lawton Benscoter won't advertise. He's so stubborn."

Spur nodded. "Maybe if you go and see him, have a talk. His long fight was with your father, not with you. You might be able to establish a friendlier attitude. He must know that he should be advertising. Might be worth a try."

Gypsy brightened. "Spur McCoy, you're a good man to have around. I'll have to show you my appreciation by cooking a dinner for you. How about tonight at my house at six-thirty."

"Miss Pinnick . . . that is, Gypsy. I'd be delighted to have dinner at your house tonight."

When they arrived at the tent, she opened the frame door held in place only by a hook and eye.

"If anyone wants to steal anything inside, all they have to do is cut a hole in the tent. It's not my tent, so I leave the door open. So far, nothing is missing."

They went in, and Spur spread the paper over a small table. There had to be some clues in these papers. All he had to do was find them.

Chapter Four

The tall man watched from his second floor window on Main Street as Spur McCoy and Gypsy Pinnick went into the tent just across the thoroughfare.

"Who the hell is he and what's he doing here in town?" the thin man asked as he turned from the window. "Especially I want to know what he's doing with Gypsy. He came in town on the stage yesterday and before dark he had talked to the lady owner of the newspaper. What the hell's going on?"

Loophole Larson glared at the man across the room from him. "I've got a lot riding on this deal. If it doesn't work because of some wild-eyed stranger who drops into town after all of our plans are made . . ."

Larson let it hang in the air as he dropped into

the leather executive chair behind his ponderous desk. The irregular shaped top was made from two huge slabs of cherry wood, polished to a mirror sheen and then varnished to a gloss. It was one of his treasures.

Across the room, J. Lawton Benscoter chuckled. "Larson, I thought you had nerves of steel, but I'm beginning to doubt it. We put this together so nothing could go wrong. You came up with the legal moves yourself. You know it's as solid as it ever was." Benscoter was nearly a foot shorter than Larson at five-seven to the lawyer's six-two.

Benscoter walked over to the chair beside the desk and gave a grunt of pain as he sat down. "Damn gout. I'd like to cut that right big toe off and throw it away. It's hot and swollen and hurts like old Billy Hell."

"Sign of high living," Larson said and scowled. "Now, what the hell do we do about this gent who is getting friendly with Miss Pinnick?"

Benscoter eased back in the chair. "Relax, Larson, relax. You'll have a coronary or catch the tremors or fly all to pieces, and we'll have to pack you off to the loony bin in Phoenix." Benscoter eased a ten cent cigar from his suit pocket, snipped off the end, then licked the outside tobacco leaves and sniffed it.

"Damn wonderful thing, a fine cigar. Enough to help a man get up in the morning just thinking about that first smoke." He lit the cigar with a match from a long thin box on the lawyer's desk. When he had blown out two or three big drags of smoke, he settled back.

"First off, Mr. Larson, I don't like this attitude you're taking. You came into this project on my recommendation, and you stand to gain your ten percent of the profits. That does not entitle you to make policy, to run off at the mouth, or demand that something be done. You carefully worked out all of the legal jargon about how to make it foolproof and workable. I'm the man who gets the spade work done, and our other friend is the third cog in the machinery who enables all of this to take place."

He stopped and took another long pull on the brown stogie. J. Lawton Benscoter turned his face upward and blew a perfect smoke ring that floated slowly toward the ten-foot ceiling, at last breaking up near the top of the room where the June heat gathered.

"To ease your mind, Larson, the man's name is Spur McCoy. He listed his work as salesman in the hotel register and showed as his employer a Denver firm I've never heard of. Not quite sure what he does, but the clerk said he makes out like he's a cowboy but has the manners and talks like an educated easterner. So, you see you have little to worry about. My guess is that he's in the printing trades and is here to talk with the lady about her printing plant. Perhaps he wants to help finance her reconstruction for a part of the ownership."

Larson snorted. "He sure as hell won't get far doing that. Two days after the fire, I suggested that we have a community owned paper. I told that pretty lady I'd be glad to set up the company and make shareholders of all those who wanted to finance her new building and equipment. She turned me down flat. Said she didn't want any partners. She wanted to be able to write any story she found. No partners, no control, strictly independent."

Benscoter nodded. "Heard about that. She's getting as pig-headed as her old man was, but she can't be as strait-laced as he was. I'm thinking of putting in an ad in her new small paper to help her along. No reason I have to fight with her—at least not yet. Might forestall any unfavorable comments for a time."

Lawson stood, went to the window again, parted the curtains and watched the tent across the way. The site had been cleaned up but not much else had been done. "I still say my advice to you a week ago is the best. Buy her out now. Offer her two thousand dollars cash and take over any outstanding bills and receivables. You're buying the name of the paper, any existing back files, what equipment has been salvaged and the paper's goodwill. That way you can put in your own editor, and no one will know that you own the paper."

Benscoter blew another smoke ring. "Yes, I thought about it. Interesting idea. Control the press and you control the people. But it would cut out the good fight that I enjoy with the press. If I'm not mistaken, the young lady and I will have a time of peace, then arrows of doubt will slant from her pages and soon we'll be back in a toe to toe battle again. I enjoy a good fight, Larson. Haven't you figured that out yet?"

"So what do we do about this Spur McCoy?"

"I've telegraphed the company in Denver. Should have an answer soon about who they are and what they sell. I didn't mention McCoy, since they might notify him about the inquiry. When we find out what he's up to, we'll know what to do."

"The man is going to be a problem. I sense it," Larson said. "Something about the way he walks, that holster tied low on his leg like he's a gunsharp.

He's no more a salesman than you are. I don't trust him, and we need to watch him."

Benscoter grunted his approval. Larson was acting dangerously near to losing his nerve on this project. This was the first time that Benscoter had needed a lawyer for one of these projects. Oh, he had worked various ploys and schemes in his time, but this would be the biggest and the best paying.

He and the sheriff would share in the profits after Larson had his ten percent. He wasn't sure of market value, but the appraised value was interesting. This scheme would net him more than he could make in another lifetime.

Benscoter heaved out of the chair. He was putting on some weight and knew it. At 51 years of age he should be given a little bit of leeway. Not that his wife appreciated it. He was still having some trouble with her in bed, and it riled him. He liked to do her when he was sure she was safe. He'd had two too many kids already, and they had not been happy experiences.

Benscoter waved at the lawyer. "Loophole, you keep one hand on your crotch now and don't lose your nerve. This is rolling along on schedule. The paper is down so that eliminates one of the problems. Now we simply carry on with the notice and nothing can go wrong. You worry too much."

The town's major mover left the lawyer's office, shuffled across the hard-packed dirt street to the boardwalk, walked four doors up from the burned-out newspaper and went into his office building. It was the only one in Pine Grove built especially for offices. On the ground floor was his real estate firm and land office. Next to it, facing the street, was Doc Johnson's office.

An outside staircase led to the second story

where his offices took up the entire floor. He'd hired a decorator to come up from Phoenix to furnish and finish the inside of his three offices.

The first was an outer reception area where Alice sat at her desk, deftly received visitors, screened those wanting to see him, and kept a list of any appointments or visitors he had for that day. Alice was 49 years-old, plump, wore spectacles and frumpy clothes and called herself an executive assistant. She was so good at her work that Benscoter paid her $40 a month, $15 more than anyone else in town doing the same kind of work earned. She was worth it.

Alice greeted him when he walked in the door. Often he went in a rear entrance down a short hallway, but this time he needed to see Alice.

"Mr. Benscoter, a Paul Wainfield was here to see you, but he had to leave to make another appointment. He'll stop back this afternoon. You have a meeting with the sheriff at noon, lunch he calls it, at the Del Rey Café. Nothing else. The mail isn't sorted yet.

"Oh, yes, the postmaster sent a note by a young lad. He'd like to see you at your convenience at his office. The note's on your desk."

"Thank you, Alice. Anything else?"

"Your first appointment is in your office. You said to send her in whenever she came."

"Yes, Alice, I'd forgotten." Benscoter smiled with warmth at Alice, went through a door marked "Private" and closed it softly. He pushed a bolt into place and turned around.

"Clarissa, sorry I'm late. Business."

Clarissa sat on a sofa that filled half of one wall. It had been specially made, the back crowded with pillows. She patted the spot beside her, and when

Benscoter sat down, she pushed her thigh against his.

"Now, J. Lawton, last time we were talking about what excites a woman, because when you sense that your partner is getting all sexy and hot and ready to go, it will affect your own desire as well." As she spoke, Clarissa unbuttoned the white blouse she wore and her breasts came into view.

"You . . . you mean I need to get her hot, so I'll get excited, too?"

"It works out that way. Now, we talked how most women just love to be kissed—long, hot, sensuous kisses with your tongue in her mouth. Some women think that when she lets your tongue into her mouth that it's like being penetrated down below. It's a signal that it's all right to enter her vagina."

The blouse hung open to her waist.

Clarissa had one hand on his thigh, and she woved it up to his crotch. She frowned slightly. "J. Lawton, didn't unbuttoning my blouse get you excited? Looking at the edge of my bare breasts doesn't help you?"

"A little. I've seen a lot of tits, Clarissa. Maybe I'm just getting old and can't get it up anymore."

"Nonsense. I know a man who is seventy-eight and still humps his wife every Thursday night. Your little problem is in your skull, not your prick." She reached up, undid his fly and worked her hand inside.

"Good, you're starting. Take off my blouse. That will help."

He slid the blouse off her shoulders, and she let it hang there, showing both her breasts.

"J. Lawton Benscoter, you've got to want to fuck before you can fuck. Most men are wild to go as soon as they see a tit. You can still perform, but you've just got to want to fuck more. Think how good it feels when you pump off and climax and the woman squeals and yells with delight. Nothing in the world better."

"Show me again."

She stripped him, then took off her own clothes and tried to teach him the best way to make love to a woman. It took him almost an hour to get a passing grade.

As they dressed she shook her head at him. "J. Lawton, what you need is more practice. I can come in three days a week if you'd like. Or better yet, you should be humping your wife twice a week. In a couple of months you'll be chasing the young girls down the street like a stud bull."

"Damn, I hope so." He took a five dollar bill from his wallet and gave it to her. "Let's try that three times a week here first—Monday, Wednesday and Friday—but make it at four in the afternoon. I work better then than mornings."

Alice nodded when Clarissa left. Alice had never said a word about the treatment sessions or about Clarissa, who worked nights at the Lucky Seven Saloon in the cribs upstairs. Clarissa always used the backstairs so no one would see her come and go.

J. Lawton dressed and combed what was left of his graying hair. He had that noon talk with the sheriff. Nothing unusual. They had been getting together for lunch now and then for eight years.

He made it on time at the Del Rey Café and waved at Sheriff Ben Willard who had claimed a table in the back. Usually they ate by the front window. Sheriff Willard looked pensive today. His pinched face seemed to spell out worry, and his pot belly touched the edge of the table.

Benscoter slid into the chair, signaled for a cup of coffee and looked at the sheriff.

"We're on schedule," he said so only the lawman could hear.

"Damn well hope so. After this is all over, some folks are gonna be looking and poking around, trying to say it was illegal."

"That's why we have Loophole. He says the fact that the paper burned down and printed only a single sheet letter-sized paper on the date we needed is a legitimate reason for not advertising. There wasn't any advertising, and it was more a letter than a newspaper.

"Loophole says we're on solid ground. He says intent is the big thing here. We turned in the ads to the newspaper and scheduled it for publication, listing all the involved parties. It wasn't our fault the advertisements never appeared. Our intent was legal. The letters were mailed registered the same day the ads were to come out. We're legal as anything can be."

"But they never were published."

"Sheriff Willard, drop it. Loophole says we're on solid ground. He had four cases when much the same thing happened down in Phoenix, and the judge ruled that the intent had been there. Circumstances out of the control of the sheriff occurred, but the law had been followed as best it could be. Forget it and be ready to do the rest of your job."

The sheriff sighed. The waitress came and took their order, then hurried away.

"I tell you everything is working out the way we want it to. Just hold tight. In a little over a week it should all be played out, and we'll both have a bundle of cash."

"Damnit, I hope so, J. Lawton. Some of them due bills go back ten years, and it's high time. Oh, damn, I guess we're into this too far to back off now."

J. Lawton's hand came down with sudden force, pinning the sheriff's arm to the table.

"Sheriff, I don't want you ever to say that again or even think it. You're in this up to your neck. Why in hell do you suppose I contributed more than half of your campaign fund the last two elections? We work together—or come a year next November, I'll get a new sheriff elected. Understand?"

The sheriff nodded. J. Lawton smiled again. It wouldn't do for the town folks to see the two most powerful men in the county having an argument.

J. Lawton had worried a little about Sheriff Willard, but he was the vital link in the chain. Without him there would be nothing. He had to be along and had done his bit so far. The end of the campaign was the most important. He had his man, and he wasn't going to let him go.

Right after lunch with the sheriff, J. Lawton walked over to the post office that operated out of the J. Lawton Benscoter General Store. The postmaster also managed the store, since the government paid little more than a modest salary for the right to be the town's mailman.

There was a wall of boxes for the mail behind a partition with a window in it. Mail was sorted alphabetically, and residents called at the window for their mail daily or when they expected something.

Jessie Ferris looked up when Benscoter came in the store. He swallowed hard and waved his boss behind the partition. Ferris was short and wiry, with a full beard he kept trimmed to half an inch.

He wore spectacles and needed dental work.

"About these registered letters. I did what you told me to, but now what am I supposed to do with them? I got the forms signed off and everything, but you didn't tell me what to do with the damn letters."

Benscoter grinned. "No big worry, Jessie. Seems to me it's getting a little chilly in here. About time to start up your heater in the back room. Them letters make damn fine kindling, don't you think? Let's take care of them right now so there won't be any misunderstanding."

"I don't know, Mr. Benscoter."

"Hell, Jessie, you done the crime already. You failed to deliver registered U.S. mail. On top of that you forged forty-seven signatures and X's on delivery chits. You can't get in any deeper, Jessie. Besides, I already paid you that one hundred dollars in advance, right? Then you have four hundred more coming when it's all over. You're bought and paid for, Jessie, so now do your duty. Let's burn up those letters and stir the damn ashes so there isn't the least little shred of evidence that they were never delivered."

Chapter Five

Secret Service Agent Spur McCoy worked over the four back issues of the *Clarion* for an hour. He found no story of any significance that he thought could lead to murder.

The way the fires had been set at both doors of the newspaper building left no doubt in his mind that someone wanted the publisher dead. Yet there had been compassion, or some other reason, because the daughter had been spared. The fire could have been set at any time, yet the killers waited until the pretty young girl had gone out for supper, a regular occurrence on Wednesday nights that half the town must know about.

Spur leaned back in the chair and laced his fingers together behind his head. What in hell had got the killers so stirred up? He watched Gypsy working at a small table nearby and thought she was as pretty as a butterfly sitting on a fresh red rose.

"You're working hard this morning, Gypsy."

"They had a town council meeting I attended and I'm just writing it up for the paper."

"You'll do another small sized edition?"

"Yes, and every week until I get the big press fixed and have enough paper and ink to print the *Clarion* in its usual size."

"Then you don't expect the people who killed your father to cause you or the paper any more trouble?"

"Not unless they think that I'm stepping on their toes. Since I don't have the slightest idea who they might be, I'll probably write something they don't like soon enough. Papa and I thought alike on most of the important issues around the county."

"What are those important issues, Gypsy?"

"Taxation for one. The county commissioners want to raise the tax base so they can build a new courthouse and pay themselves a salary. Most of us don't want that. Things are moving along just fine."

"What else?"

"The local school district. It's a taxing institution and gets voter approval for new funds. Our schoolhouse is a shame. We need a new one built out of brick or stone so it will last a while. Many older people without children won't vote for more school taxes.

"Then the Methodists are trying to get a no fire-arms law in the city limits. That's so nobody can carry a gun off their own property without a county permit. They say ten men and one woman were shot dead in the city last year because of the flagrant misuse of firearms."

"That one must make everyone unhappy one

way or the other. I'd just as soon keep wearing my side arm if it's all right with you."

"The paper hasn't taken a position on the gun law yet. It may be put up to a vote of the people, and my guess is it would be voted down."

"Gypsy, there must be something else brewing, something bigger than what you told me about. I'm thinking it must be something that would involve large sums of money, a plan or a scheme or a project that would bring a great deal of money to someone here in town. An increase in taxes would mean a lot of money, but it would all go into the county coffers. That can't be it."

Gypsy wrinkled her brow and rubbed her chin. "I just can't think of anything that would fit your description."

"Maybe that's part of my problem. What we're talking about might not be public knowledge, yet somehow your father found out about it and was ready to break the story. I wish we could have gone through his desk and files. He just might have made some notes on a story this big."

A noise at the doorway brought Spur's head around. He relaxed when he saw a tall man in a business suit duck and come in.

"Well, Mr. Larson," Gypsy said, "how do you like the new offices of the *Clarion?*"

Larson was in his early forties, slender, over six feet and with that lean, hungry look Spur had always associated with coyotes on a sparse range.

"Not quite as fancy as your old place. How's the battle going?"

"Hard, working on getting the press into operation. Until then I'll put out the small paper."

"Any room for ads yet? One of my clients is interested."

"No, I can't offer the space or the circulation, so I decided not to run ads until the regular paper comes out. I'm losing money, but it seems the only fair way."

"Highly public spirited of you, Miss Pinnick." Larson turned and looked at Spur.

"Oh, I'm sorry," Gypsy said. "Loophole Larson, this is Spur McCoy."

Spur nodded at the man. "Loophole . . . that mean you're a lawyer?"

Larson laughed. "It does. I gained a reputation for finding holes in the system and in contracts and the moniker just stuck to me. I decided to utilize it."

Spur took a closer look at the lawyer. He must have seen the other small paper and knew there wasn't any advertising. Was he just curious about what was inside the tent, or did he have some other motive? It was easy to be suspicious of everyone in this situation. Spur could not read the man as friend or foe. A lawyer in a town this size would carry considerable weight. He'd see what he could learn about Larson.

"I hear we may have an old-fashioned barn raising one of these days to put up your new building," Larson said.

"Only a dream right now," Gypsy said and grinned. "Unless, Mr. Larson, you want to donate about two hundred dollars worth of lumber and supplies."

He chuckled. "Not right now, lass, but I'm a fair hand with a hammer and saw when the time comes." He looked around again, then nodded. "Well, I better be about my duties. Let me know if there's anything I can do. I understand your father had no insurance. It's expensive but sure can be handy." He looked at Spur. "Good meeting you, Mr. McCoy. I better be off." He smiled at Gypsy and hurried out the framed door.

Spur frowned at Gypsy. "What do you suppose that was all about?"

Gypsy brushed her long hair away from her eyes. "I have no idea. I've always got along with Larson well. He's the city attorney when they need one to interpret the laws and such. Seems friendly enough."

"Has he ever advertised in the paper?"

"No, but he does place an ad for a client now and then." She paused and studied him. "You're still coming to supper tonight?"

"Wouldn't miss it. A home cooked meal. I'd juggle three eggs and stand on my head for that."

Gypsy laughed, and he could see traces of the little girl in her. "Good, I'll hold you to that tonight." She moved from the small table to the type case, pulled out a drawer, and began picking up individual letters and placing them in a holder to set the story in type.

He watched, then moved over for a closer view. "You know where each of those letters is situated in that drawer."

She nodded not missing a letter as she spoke. "It's called learning the case or the drawer. All letters are in the same position no matter what font or kind of type you're setting. That makes it easier. Supposedly the letters are arranged so the ones used most often like i's and e's and a's are closer to the hand. The x and z are way out on the edge."

"Have you thought about any money issue that somebody would get murderous about?"

She shook her head, her long black hair rippling

down her back where it hung to just below her waist. "Not a thing. This isn't a rich town. No railroad coming, no gold mine discovered. Not even silver. I can't imagine what could be worth that much here in Pine Grove."

"What about the timber? I see a lot of pine trees around here."

"Good try, Spur, but the pines are not all that big and not the best for lumber. They make a fine fire, and the young ones are good for fence posts and telegraph poles. Outside of that, not the best money crop."

"Maybe I'm on the wrong trail here. What about some personal vendetta someone had for your father."

"Papa was intense and single-minded, but he really liked people. When he got angry it was because someone was taking advantage of a weaker person. He said the *Clarion* was here for the common man, for the little people who don't have lawyers or money to speak for them. Papa was an optimist. I do think the paper has been a help in the past and will be again, to keep the elected officials honest and to stand up for the common folk."

"I think you're an idealist like your father," Spur said. "I better wander your town, try to get to know more about it. Maybe I'll stumble on something to help us. We probably will never find the men who started the fires, but the man we want is the one who paid them to do so. When he find some big money scheme, we'll find the real killer."

Gypsy blinked rapidly, and when he went to her and put his arm around her, she dropped her head on his chest. He held her tightly.

"I didn't mean to upset you, Gypsy. You're a

strong young lady. I have great hopes for you."

She looked at him, wiped the tears from her eyes, reached up and kissed his cheek.

"Thank you, kind gentleman. I do need a good hug now and then. That should keep me working for the rest of the day." He let her go and she stepped back. "Maybe you could do that again one of these times." Her face was in repose, so vulnerable and open it made his heart pound. The mood passed and she smiled.

"Maybe after dinner, if I do a good job and you're off your guard," she said grinning.

He waved and hurried out the door. This was a girl a man could learn to like so much he wouldn't want to leave her. That kind of a relationship was not in his plans. He walked up the street, wondering what in this small town high in the Arizona mountains held such a secret that it had cost a man his life and his newspaper.

J. Lawton Benscoter stared at the telegram in his hand. "TO: T. L. BENSCOTER, PINE GROVE, ARIZONA. THE FIRM OF SOLOMON AND SONS, OUTFITTERS AND GENERAL HARDWARE, DENVER, HAS NO OUTSIDE SALESMEN. IF ANY FRAUD IS COMMITTED THERE BY IMPOSTER, NOTIFY LOCAL AUTHORITIES. HELP US PROTECT OUR GOOD NAME. J. SOLOMON SENDING."

Benscoter read the wire again, tore it into small pieces and dropped them in the waste basket. So, Spur McCoy was not who he said he was. Now the task was to determine who he was and what he wanted in Pine Grove. Damn bad timing with just a week to go until the project would be complete. His greatest coup in

30 years, and now it all might hang in the balance.

After this paid off, he could sit back and relax, hire some bright young man to run things for him, and move to Phoenix where they had more of the easy life. Yes, in Phoenix he could keep tabs on things up here and yet have some of the luxuries.

It was near the middle of the afternoon, a time when most men would not be in their hotel rooms. Benscoter went to the Pine Grove Hotel, nodded at the clerk and went up the stairs to room 212.

No one was in the hall. He checked the door. Locked. He used his master key, stepped inside and relocked the door. Then he turned the key halfway around so no other key could be inserted to unlock the panel.

He searched the room quickly and deftly. Unless he left some special signals, McCoy wouldn't know anyone had been here. In the bottom of a leather traveling bag he found the spare set of identification that McCoy always carried.

Now Benscoter read the card and accompanying letter that had been signed by William Wood himself. Even Benscoter knew who William Wood was in Washington politics. He scowled as he returned the material to its rightful place, put back everything else as it had been and stepped to the door. Silently he unlocked it and cracked it open. No one in the hall.

Benscoter stepped out and locked the door, then walked down the hall wondering what to do. He had a federal lawman on his hands, a Secret Service man empowered by the federal government to investigate any crimes against the nation, any interstate crime, and any problem where a local law enforcement officer requested aid and assistance. What the hell should he do now?

Benscoter thought about it as he sipped a shot of whiskey at the Blue Goose Saloon which he owned, though few in town realized it. He now owned about half the retail establishments in town, and he wanted them all.

What in hell should he do about Spur McCoy? He could hire any one of half a dozen men in town to blow McCoy's brains out in a dark alley tonight. But would that be the best solution? It would solve the short term problem, but would it open up the way for a half dozen federal lawmen to come trooping in?

Larson was the legal expert; he would talk to him about it. McCoy was sniffing around the newspaper and the girl. Was he here to dig into the fire and the chance that it had not been an accident as the county coroner had determined? Now that would be a problem.

At least the men who struck the matches would never be found. They were well past Phoenix now and on their way to San Francisco. Still something could be turned up that would derail the big project.

The only problem there he could see was Jessie Ferris. He was tied in, incriminated already, but that might not be enough. Benscoter would watch the bearded little man closely. No one was going to foul up this project. Ferris was expendable. He had done his part and could be eliminated any time. In fact, that would be best, making one less witness, one less trouble spot that could blow the whole project right over the moon. He'd think about Jessie. The man was of no use anymore and presented a sizeable liability. Did the liability outweigh the risk? That was the problem Benscoter would have to decide soon.

But first, McCoy. What the hell should he do about this federal lawman breathing down his neck?

Chapter Six

Spur McCoy had walked through the small town of Pine Grove from one end to the other, all three blocks of it, and he had prowled the back streets and alleys. Now he sat in the Home Café sipping a cup of coffee. He had an hour yet before he was to show up for supper at the small white house where Gypsy Pinnick lived.

He had learned little this afternoon. The people he talked to had no idea of any big money plot afoot. Most of them joked about it. Said the town fathers had the gravy train by getting five dollars a meeting for doing almost nothing. Nobody wanted to talk about the anti-gun law except one Methodist who was all for it.

"My cousin came near to death last year when two drunks decided to have an old-fashioned shoot out on Main Street. Both were so potted they couldn't hit the ground and both took five shots at each other. My cousin was a half block away and caught a round in his chest. Could have killed him, but it didn't."

Spur took a pull at the coffee. It was a fair brew, stronger than he liked it but good enough for now. He'd been in town for a little over 24 hours and already the pot was cooking. He had spent a lot of time around the *Clarion* tent hoping that would make somebody nervous, but so far there was no payoff on that ploy.

A land grab? How can you get land for free in a place like this? Most of the surrounding countryside and mountains were federal property. Much of it would revert to the state if and when Arizona gained enough population and met the other requirements to become a state. A land grab didn't seem reasonable, although about 50 sections of land in these mountains should produce enough timber to make the deal worthwhile.

That would require going through congress and the Department of the Interior. There also were several large Indian reservations that were off limits to any kind of land deal.

He finished his coffee, put a nickel on the counter and headed for Gypsy's house. He had no illusions about taking her to bed tonight. She was the kind of lady you took home to mother and put a wedding band on her finger before you lifted her skirts—and rightly so. She was a lady.

For a moment he compared her to Flo Benscoter who was a good time girl who liked sex as much as men did and didn't care where she got it. Flo was a fast tumble in bed; Gypsy was a long term commitment of marriage and family.

He knocked on the door, and it popped open at once. Gypsy stood there, smiling and gorgeous. She must have brushed her waist-length raven-black hair a hundred times. She had trimmed the bangs across her forehead, and her soft brown eyes glowed with a happiness he hadn't seen there before.

"Welcome to the Pinnick place," she said. "Your dinner isn't quite ready but you're welcome to help me finish it in the kitchen." When she reached up and kissed his cheek, for just a moment her breasts brushed his chest.

"Now you're properly welcomed. Do you know how to mash potatoes?"

A few minutes later she watched him with delight. "A little more salt and a spoon full of butter," she directed. "If you were a prospective beau I wouldn't let you within twenty feet of my kitchen. Oh, it's quite simple. I'm not all that good at cooking. Actually Papa did most of the cooking after Mama died. He was good at it. I told him he should open a restaurant."

Spur listened, delighted to hear her running on this way. It told him that she was more than a little nervous having him here for a social occasion rather than work.

She chattered on for another five minutes until he held up his hands.

"Hey, usually you don't talk on and on this way. That tells me you're nervous, and I wish you wouldn't be. This is a business dinner, not social at all. Will that help you relax a little?"

She took a long breath and nodded. "I guess . . . I guess I just sort of got myself all nervous and bothered. Sorry."

Spur chuckled. "It's interesting to see you this

way. You're as pretty as a speckled fawn, and right now about as skitterish. Look, Gypsy, I'm not here to court or woo or seduce you. It's just a friendly little dinner between friends. Nothing to worry about."

He held up the crockery bowl with the potatoes mashed and whipped to a creamy white. "Here is the proof, a topnotch batch of mashed potatoes ready for the table."

Gypsy laughed and brought to the table fried chicken, gravy, carrots, peas and some boiled cabbage.

As they sat down to eat, she reached over and touched his hand. "Thanks for understanding. If it's business, I stay all business, but on the social scene, I get all giddy like a sixteen year-old having her first kiss."

Spur went through the food like a starved man, and she relaxed more. They talked about the problem of the big scam but neither of them had any ideas.

"It can't be mountain land or gold or oil or timber," he said. "I just don't see what else is here that could build up this kind of anger against your father."

"It must be something. I'm sure it wasn't some kind of a personal vendetta. Folks around here face off and scream at each other, and if they're young enough they throw a few punches and the problem is worked out. I just don't understand."

Spur knew she was right. This young lady not only had a nice body and beautiful face, she was smart as well. When the dinner was finished, he insisted on helping her clean up and wash the dishes.

"I'll dry," he said. "I'm best at that."

Twenty minutes later they settled down in the living room.

"Sometimes it seems strange here. Now this is my house. I grew up here and seen a lot of changes. Sometimes I still can't be sure that Papa is gone. I figure he's working late at the paper and he'll come home hungry as a wolverine and I won't have any supper for him."

She looked away, rubbed her eyes for a moment and then turned back to him.

"One thing, I wish I had more self-confidence. Sometimes I'm not sure what I'm doing is right."

Spur grinned and then chuckled. "Gypsy, if you had any more self-confidence you'd be mayor and ready to run for governor. You're doing just fine."

"Well, how nice. Thank you for those fine words. I do know one thing. When I get married it will be for love, and because the man is the kind who will look upon me as a partner and not as something else he owns. My future husband will accept the idea that I am a whole person, that I have the right to run my newspaper after we're married, and that he won't own any of the paper or have anything to do with it—unless he's a professional newspaperman who knows what he's doing."

Spur stood. "Gypsy, even with a list of requirements like that, I'd say you won't last another year before some lucky man waltzes you right down the aisle into matrimony. Now, I thank you for the fine meal. I appreciate it. I better be getting back to my room and figure out what to do tomorrow."

She walked him to the door where she touched his shoulder. He turned toward her. "Spur, would you kiss me please?"

He smiled and bent and kissed her lips, softly

and gently. They parted after a few seconds and she gave a little sigh.

"That was fine, but let's try it again." This time her hands came around his neck, and she pressed hard against his chest. The kiss was fire and ice and lasted longer than he expected. When she at last pulled away from his lips, she clung to him, her face against his shoulder.

She sighed again, then stepped back and laughed ruefully. "I know that was not a smart thing to do. But when I'm around you, I'm not always smart, especially when you're kissing me. I have been kissed before in case you're wondering. I enjoyed it. Perhaps again sometime. Now, like you said, you do have to go."

She opened the screen door and let him outside, then closed it and looked through it. "Oh, yes, Spur McCoy, now that was a kiss to remember. Will I see you tomorrow?"

"I'll stop by your tent, for sure." He turned and walked away with her watching him through the screen.

Spur lifted his brows when he was halfway down the dark block toward Main. Gypsy was a lot more woman than he had thought at first. Somehow he figured she was 19. A lot of suppressed desire flooded out in that last kiss. He wondered if she had ever made love. His first response was no, but as he thought about it, she might have come on too strong to some young man not able to control himself. Could have happened.

It was really none of his business, just curiosity. He pushed it out of his mind. What was left to do tomorrow? He'd covered most of the bases here. He had no leads at all on the murder. He could help organize the barn raising for the new building, but she would still be $1,000 short to start up the *Clarion* again.

Just this side of Main Street, he saw two men in the shadows of the hardware store. They probably would be gone by the time he got there. Then he was near the hardware, and the two men stood 20 feet ahead blocking his path.

"You boys looking for trouble?" he asked stopping ten feet from them.

"Not if you're not," one said. "Give us your wallet and your pocket watch and you're free to go."

"Not a chance." He started to draw, but too late he sensed the loop settle over him and the rope jerk tight, pinning his arms to his side. One of the men jerked the lariat forward with all of his weight, and Spur staggered a step, then stumbled and went down and slid through the dust of the street another three feet before he stopped.

One of the men knelt on top of him, slid the six-gun from leather and pounded his fist into Spur's stomach.

After that neither of the two said a word. The rope held tight as they got him to his feet, looped the rope around him again and tied it off tight. The fists came with practiced ease against his belly, then his face. He took three more shots to his stomach before he saw the opening he wanted. One of the men in front of him backed up half a step for a longer swing.

Spur kicked upward with his right foot as hard as he could. His hard leather toe caught the man along the inside of his left thigh and rocketed upward, crashing into his scrotum, driving it upward against his pelvic bones, crushing both testicles, dumping the man backwards where he lay screaming in terrible pain.

"Oh, shit!" the other tough said and turned and ran down the street. Spur worked at the knots in the rope, and before the man writhing on the ground could stand, Spur had the rope off and found his gun where they had tossed it. He put the loop around the tough's neck and drew it tight.

"Get to your feet or I'll kick you again," Spur snarled. His belly hurt like fire, and he knew he had lost some skin off his nose and under his eye. He'd have a black eye by morning. No matter, this might be his first break on the case.

The attacker shrieked in pain as he stood, then he walked spraddle-legged so he wouldn't move his wounded testicles.

Next to the first saloon, where lamplight spilled onto the boardwalk, Spur pushed the wounded man against the wall and doubled his fist under the man's wild eyes.

"Who hired you?"

"Nobody, broke, needed some cash."

"Not a chance. You followed me to the lady's house, waited for me to come out and challenged me. You're not a range rat. You both knew exactly what you were doing and how to make it hurt the most without killing me. You've got ten seconds, then my fist hits your crotch as hard as I can swing."

"Nobody hired us."

Spur held him with one hand at his throat and fisted his right and swung it back. Just before he started his fist toward the man's crotch, he broke.

"No, no! God, no, not again. All right, I'll tell you. Don't hit me again."

"Who, where?"

"Don't know his name. Asked us if we could use a rope and didn't have any problem with pounding somebody around a little. Paid us twenty dollars."

"Who was he?"

"Don't know him. Bear of a man, over six feet, wide shoulders, red hair, beer belly. Talked with a lisp."

"Where did you meet him?"

"A saloon, don't remember which one."

"You've got twenty seconds to remember the name."

It came at once as the man's eyes turned from side to side as if searching for help. "The Blue Goose Saloon. Down the street a ways."

"Good." Spur pulled the noose tighter around the man's neck until he gurgled from lack of air, then Spur slackened it. "You better go see Doc Johnson about them nuts of yours. They might be mashed up a little. Leastwise you won't want to look at a naked woman for at least three months."

Spur pushed him down the street and went off toward the Blue Goose. A man that big couldn't be hard to find in a town the size of Pine Grove.

The big man wasn't in the Blue Goose. Spur hung around for an hour, drank a cold beer, watched some poker and some faro. He didn't play, but checked every man who came in or went out. The big bear man was not there. Not a redhead in the place. Spur wondered how his own face looked. He could stand the pain in his belly, but his face would show tomorrow.

He went back to the hotel and looked in the mirror. A nasty bruise showed under his right eye and his nose had lost half an inch of skin. He went to the hotel kitchen and talked them out of a six-inch square of river ice and took it upstairs. He broke up some of the ice, wrapped it in a towel and held it against his cheek.

The ice should help reduce the swelling and with any luck would drive some of the blood out of the tissue. He painted his nose with some ointment he had for such small injuries and stared at his face in the mirror again. Tomorrow everyone would know he'd been in a brawl.

In certain quarters, that might prove to be an asset. His first task was to find the redheaded bear. Somebody would know him, maybe the man at the post office. He saw every person in town on a regular basis. Yes, good choice.

Spur stripped down and tried to sleep, but his gut hurt too much. He got up and smoked a thin brown stogie, watching the saloons out his window. It was a quiet night without a single gunfight, and only one fisticuffs erupted all the way to the street out of a saloon.

A little after eleven he checked his watch with a match. Hopefully he'd sleep for a while before morning. A few minutes later a knock sounded on his door. He drew his six-gun from its leather and went to the wall next to the door.

"Who is it?"

"A friend with gifts," Flo said. He let the hammer down gently on the round and unlocked the door.

"Were you sleeping?" Flo asked.

"No. I'll light the lamp. I'm not decent."

"Good, I won't be either for long."

He lit the lamp, put on the chimney and turned down the wick to a steady flame.

Flo looked at him wearing only his short cotton underdrawers.

"You look fine to me. Maybe a little over-dressed." She held out a sack. "Look inside."

He found a bottle of wine, three kinds of cheese and three apples.

"I figured we might get hungry after."

"Look at my face," he told her.

She did. "Tsk, fighting again. Naughty boy. I should spank you." She looked at him for a reaction.

"Not tonight, sexy lady." He told her about the two saddle tramps who had jumped him. "Somebody in your fine little town doesn't like me. Oh, do you know a big bear of a man over six feet who has red hair?"

"Sure, everybody knows Red Kenny. He's one of the guys who beat you up?"

"No, he hired them."

"Oh, gawd!"

"What?"

"Red has worked for my husband from time to time. He's good at a lot of things, kind of a handyman around town. Works for a lot of people."

"Know where he lives?"

"Not the slightest idea. Now, let's get naked and get down to doing some wild, strange and wonderful fucking."

Spur pointed to the bruise marks on his belly.

"I'm having enough trouble just breathing tonight, Flo. Better postpone our party until I'm feeling better."

"You just lay on your back. You don't even have to move."

He reached out and fondled her breasts through the thin dress. "Not a chance, lady. Have you ever been beaten up? No fun, and it takes some recuperation time. Tomorrow night about the same time?"

She kissed him, gently felt his crotch, then picked up her sack of food and went to the door.

"Don't do anything foolish with Red. He outweighs you."

Spur held up his Colt .45 which he hadn't put back in leather.

"Probably, but he doesn't outweigh this."

"Oh, gawd, you men and your toys." She turned, slipped out the door and closed it after her. He locked it and put a chair under the knob.

It was a long night but he finally fell asleep.

Chapter Seven

When morning came, it took Spur McCoy five minutes to get out of bed. He couldn't remember being so sore or weary. The dozen blows had left a lasting impression. His first try to get out of bed as usual resulted in a searing pain in his gut and dropped him back on the mattress.

After remembering the pounding he took, he rolled over and pushed himself up with his hands, then sat down on the edge of the bed. The room spun for a moment, then righted itself. Spur took a long breath of air and let it out slowly. His face hurt, his belly hurt, even his knees hurt. He was getting too old to be beaten up that way. Next time he'd draw first, no more damn lariat around his torso pinning his hands at his sides.

Spur reached his pants and pulled them on both feet, then knew he had to stand up to finish putting them on. He stood slowly, kept his balance and pulled up the brown town pants. His body shrieked and he groaned, but he maintained his balance. The shirt was harder to get into. Damn but he was getting soft. He'd have to pick a fight a week just to stay in shape.

By the time he finished dressing and walked six steps to the mirror, he felt a little better. Then he looked at his face. The bruise under his left eye had extended upward giving him a beauty of a black eye. The scrape on his nose had sheened over with a layer of protective scab.

He'd live, but he'd be hurting for a few days.

Shaving was a chore, but once it was done he looked forward to breakfast and then a talk with the county sheriff. Most elected lawmen have a keen idea of what's going on in their area. He hoped he hit a good one.

At breakfast in the dining room below, the waitress looked at him and frowned, then took his order without any questions. He had walked into the dining room holding himself tightly, sat down with great care and leaned back before he could relax. It paid off. The bacon and French toast and a side of applesauce were good, and he poured on the hot syrup and layered on butter and ate like he was getting ready for a marathon.

Just before nine that morning, Spur walked with less and less difficulty into the sheriff's office and asked to see the top man. After a quick conference between two deputies, one went to a door and knocked.

Spur had no idea what to expect when he walked into the man's private office. Ben Willard did not look like the ideal sheriff. He was on the thin side but with a bulging belly and a pinched face. He did not wear a gun or gunbelt. Willard pushed a paper aside and looked at his visitor.

"Don't believe I know you," Sheriff Willard said. There was no warmth in his voice or attitude, only a steely eyed inquiry.

Spur took out his identification card with the silver shield on the back of it and handed it to the lawman.

Sheriff Willard read the card, looked at the shield and then read the card again.

"Secret Service? Never heard of it. Card says you're a federal lawman with jurisdiction in every state and territory. Noticed you around town for a couple of days. What you interested in here in Pine Grove?"

"The death of Andrew Weston Pinnick. How did your office list the death?"

"Pinnick, the publisher of our weekly newspaper. Coroner found no wrong doing or suspicious acts and listed the death as accidental due to fire."

"As I understand it, there were signs of coal oil being used on the only two doors to the building to start the fire. How could you or the coroner possibly decide that the coal oil and the matches to light the fluid both came to be there at the same time accidentally?"

"Coroner called it an accidental death, and I go along with his verdict. I don't go hunting trouble."

"You don't go hunting murderers either, Sheriff Willard. Pinnick was murdered by persons unknown. It's your job to find who they are and prosecute them. I strongly suggest that you reopen the case and try diligently to find the two men who started those fires, and just as important find the man who hired the killers.

"If you don't do this, Sheriff, I'll file an official complaint with the United States Attorney General as well as with the Territorial Attorney General, who I'm sure will have a team of investigators up here within three days."

The sheriff stood and walked around the room, stared out his window and then came back to his desk. He sat down and shook his head.

"No sir, I don't believe the Territorial Attorney General will come up here. This is strictly a local problem, and he don't mess in local affairs lessen he has to."

"Sheriff, this is a matter of the violation of Pinnick's constitutional rights, both a local and a federal matter. It involves not only the illegal death of Pinnick, but the violation of his rights to exercise the freedom of the press. That's why both attorney generals will be extremely interested in this case, once I present it to them."

"Freedom of the press. Nobody told him he couldn't print what he wanted to."

"It's hard to print anything once you're dead, Sheriff, which you are well-aware of. Now, I'd like to see your file and all applicable papers and orders on Pinnick's death."

"We don't got no files on it. No cause. Coroner done his report and showed it to me and put it in his files. If you want to see files, go see Doc Johnson. He's the coroner."

The sheriff stood. "Now that's the end of it. You do whatever you want. This office has closed the case, and now I'd like you to close the door when you leave. This conversation is at an end."

Spur remained seated. "Sheriff Willard, I'll leave when I'm through with my business here. I've seen several lawmen like you before—highhanded, self important, undertrained for the tough job they have, unbending. Let me remind you of something. Every territorial constitution is patterned for the territory by the federal government.

"In each is a provision for the Territorial Attorney General to remove any local sheriff, town marshal, police chief or other local law enforcement officer whether elected, appointed or hired, in case of malfeasance in office or other just cause when it is in the interests of the people in that community. Sheriff Willard, don't believe that it can't happen here. I'd advise that you reopen the Pinnick case and start tracking down the two men who set those fires and the man who hired them. You have twenty-four hours to get the investigation under way."

Spur stood, turned sharply and, without any word or gesture of farewell, left the room and walked back to the street. He felt damn good again. That sheriff would be no help in his work here. In fact he could be a hinderance.

The man was not only uncooperative but was downright hostile. Was he only angry because a federal lawman was in his jurisdiction, or was it something deeper?

By that time, the saloons were open. Spur walked into the Blue Goose and looked around. A dozen men were there. Half looked to be out of work cowboys, miners or drifters. Two dark-suited business men huddled in a conference over coffee at a back table. One game of draw poker had just started.

Spur bought a beer and watched the poker game. He refused an offer to join in. His mention of lack of funds stilled their interest in his participation.

Red Kenny was not around, but Spur figured he'd give it two hours. He was on his second beer when the redhead came in the back door.

Spur watched him as he talked to the barman, then went to a back table and sat down. Spur got up and stood across the poker table from Kenny.

"Red, you and I got some talking to do. Let's go out back."

"Who the hell are you?" the big man at the table asked. He dropped his hand below the table and Spur drew his .45 so fast the redhead scowled.

"What the hell? I can talk. No hogs leg needed. Let's talk right here first. What about?"

"You know damn well what about. My name is Spur McCoy, and you hired two saddle tramps last night to beat me up and slice me open. I don't like that."

"Afraid you have the wrong man. If I wanted you smashed up a little, I'd do that job myself."

"Why didn't you? Who hired you to hire the tramps? You're not smart enough to work up some big scheme, you're just a cog in the wheel somewhere. Who hired you?"

"Nobody. If you still want to settle this, we can move out to the alley like you said. Then no bystanders get hurt."

Spur wondered what his ploy was. He'd denied hiring the two thugs, so what more could he prove? Spur nodded, keeping the six-gun leveled on the man. "Yeah, let's go outside where I can cut you down to size a little easier, without breaking up the furniture."

Red stood with no sudden movements and kept his hand well away from the six-gun on his hip as they walked to the back door. Once there, Red went out first, then slammed the door backwards against Spur and darted into the alley.

Spur kicked the door open but stayed against the wall. Three shots jolted into the heavy wooden door as it swung out and one came through the opening. All missed Spur. He ducked, kicked the door open again and fired around the side. Spur caught one man moving from a box to the side of a building and hit him in the thigh. He went down screeching.

By that time the apron from the bar was at the back door with the sawed-off shotgun he kept to tame down fights.

"What the hell's going on back here?" he demanded, holding the shotgun ready.

"Somebody in the alley started shooting at me when I started out the door," Spur said. "Damn unfriendly town you got here. Think I'll use the front door before they run around there." Spur reloaded the empty chambers in his Colt, holstered it and walked through the saloon to the front door. Nobody tried to stop him, and no guns barked as he went out the swinging doors to the street.

He leaned against the store front next door for a minute to gather his thoughts. He didn't get far with Red Kenny, but he knew there would be another meeting with that bear of a man. In the meantime, he'd check out all possibilities. Maybe he'd had more instructions from the general in Washington D.C.

Spur pushed away from the store front and walked across the street to the Pine Grove Hotel.

A quick look in his box showed a message. The room clerk handed it to him, and Spur saw it was a plain envelope, not a telegram. Inside he found a message on lined paper.

"Spur McCoy. Understand you're a federal lawman. I know why you're here. I know what they are up to. I'll give you all the details on the scheme if you promise me total protection and that no charges will be filed against me and no public revelation made of my small part in this swindle. Come to the old stage stop about six miles out of town on the road north toward Flag at two P.M. today. I'll be waiting." The note had no signature, only the initials, J.F.

Spur checked his pocket watch and saw it was slightly after ten o'clock. Plenty of time. He always liked to get to a meeting like this well ahead of schedule to check out the lay of the land and to watch the other party arrive.

He had a thick roast beef sandwich at the Home Café, then rented a horse from the livery, borrowed a repeating rifle and a box of rounds and headed out the north road. It wound along a ridge line for several miles, and he saw the old swing station a mile before he came to it. The time was a little before one o'clock so he'd have a wait.

He stopped a quarter of a mile from the burned-out remains of the swing station. There was most of a barn left, part of the cabin, a well house and what might have been a chicken coop. Fire had gutted most of it except the barn. Might be a good spot to hole up and wait for anyone coming up the road. Loose boards on the upper part of the barn would give him a fine view down the road toward town.

As he turned the bay mare and moved toward the barn, he saw a glint of metal to the left behind a small rise and a pair of pine trees. Automatically he grabbed the rifle out of the boot and dove off the bay.

Just as he dove he felt a bullet whip through the air where his head had been a fraction of a second before. The sound of the shot came almost on top of the bullet and with it came another pair of shots. He hit the dirt on his hands, did a shoulder roll and flattened out in a small drainage ditch at the side of the wagon road.

Spur heard his horse screaming and saw her go down, shot at least twice. Then the sound of more shots came from the half-burned barn. He was out of sight of the gunman in the pine trees, but the one in the barn could see half of him. A bullet slammed into the dirt near his left leg, hit a rock and ricocheted off with a nasty whine.

Spur pulled his leg to the left out of the line of fire. He lifted up and sent one round into the barn's second floor about where he figured the gunsharp would be, but there was no reaction.

The gun from the trees blasted again twice, and this time one round came close enough to make Spur gasp. He screamed as if in sudden pain and then let the screams grow weaker and weaker until they faded out. He drew his six-gun, held it by his side and waited.

The old decoy game might work. He heard boots crunching on the road before he saw anyone. He waited, his eyes wide open in a motionless stare at the spot where the man should appear. It was all Spur could do to keep his eyeballs still as a gunman came in view, still holding the rifle aimed at Spur.

A voice came from far off, and the man turned his head for a fraction of a second and shouted something. Spur lifted the six-gun and fired.

The rifleman's finger triggered a round automatically. The round jolted through Spur's left forearm halfway down. Spur bit his lip to hold in the pain. He had seen the rifleman slam backwards from the force of the heavy .45 round.

Now Spur edged up from the ditch he lay in and looked at the roadway. A man lay there without moving. Spur had had little chance to aim, but now he saw that the round had evidently entered on an upward course under the rifleman's chin and took half of his skull off.

The rifle by the pines spoke again, and Spur slid back into the ditch to protect himself. He rose up and returned two rounds into the trees, then dropped down. This time there was no return fire.

Now it was waiting time. One man dead, his own horse dead, one more rifleman in the trees. Would he fight, or wasn't that in his plan? Maybe he figured he could cut down Spur from long distance in the deadly crossfire and go collect his blood money.

While waiting, Spur tended to his left arm. The bullets had penetrated an inch and a half of his arm but missed the bone. He used his handkerchief as a pad and his neckerchief to bind it up. He covered the wounds on both sides of his forearm and figured the tight bandage should stop the bleeding.

With his teeth, he tore the end of the kerchief so he could tie the two ends around his wrist and hold the bandage on tight.

After what Spur figured was 15 minutes, he lifted up again and fired into the pine trees. There was no response. It could mean the ambusher was gone. Knowing that kind of person, Spur figured there was little chance he would still be waiting for a chance to finish his job.

Spur looked at his rented bay, lying on the ground not moving. She must be dead. He eyed the barn. The two could have left their mounts there or in the trees behind the swing station. He got up, carried the rifle and six-gun and ran flat out toward the barn.

The first few steps were the worst, but he heard no shots, and soon he finished the 200 yards to the barn. Behind the burned-out relic he found where two horses had been tied. One mount remained. He checked the barn, then what was left of the cabin. Nobody was there, dead or alive.

He wondered now if the note had been an honest one. It could all have been a simple ploy to get him out where they could kill him. On the other hand it might have been an honestly conceived notion of this J.F. to get out of some kind of conspiracy and illegal operation.

If so, the boss of the operation must have caught him writing it or delivering it and used the note as a way to eliminate McCoy. If so, then J.F. was little better than a walking corpse—if he was still alive.

The initials might not have stood for anyone in particular, just a way to bring more credibility to the note. Either way, he'd find out soon enough.

Spur mounted the remaining horse, rode out to where his bay lay dead and pulled off the saddle and bridle. He perched them on the back of his mount and rode for town. He didn't use the easy track of the wagon road. Instead he angled off the road down a canyon and stayed a half mile off the road to be sure that the unsuccessful bushwhacker didn't get another shot at him. The six mile ride gave him lots of time to think about the case.

Chapter Eight

Just after four o'clock that afternoon, Spur turned the horse in at the livery. He said his horse had hit a gopher hole and went down, so he had to shoot it. He tried to convince the owner that the horse he brought back was as good as the one he left with.

"Besides you get a fifteen dollar saddle and bridle thrown in," Spur said. He didn't explain why he brought back another horse, and the livery man wasn't all that interested. He soon was convinced of the wisdom of the deal and charged Spur a dollar for the use of the rifle and the cartridges.

Next stop was the county coroner and medic, Doc Johnson, who had fairly new offices in the Benscoter building. The sawbones was in his sixties, spry and sharp-tongued. He stared at the open wound and nodded.

"Rifle wound, not a handgun. Seen a lot of them

in my time. Supposed to report such to the sheriff, but he don't even want me to anymore. He don't seem to be paying a whole lot of attention lately to his job."

The medic cleaned out both wounds and applied some antiseptic solution that hurt like fire. Then he put on some salve and small pads over the wounds and wrapped it tight enough to keep everything in place.

"Don't use that arm for at least a week. The slug missed the bone, but not by much. Got some major muscles in there with big holes in them."

Spur nodded. "I can do that, Doc. I have a question for you. Your report says that Andrew Pinnick's death was accidental due to fire. Did you do any investigation or hold a hearing before making that determination?"

"You're sounding like some damn lawyer, son. Fact is I went on what the sheriff and the deputies told me. Time they got there the whole damn building was on fire. Bucket brigade couldn't even hold down the smoke, let alone put out the blaze. Better get that pumper truck or this whole wooden town will burn down one of these days. Hell, no, I didn't do no investigation. They don't pay me enough to hold a real coroner's inquest, if that's what you're thinking about."

"Did anyone tell you that those first on the scene smelled coal oil at both the front and the back doors, and later on cans were found that could have held two gallons of coal oil each?"

"You don't say?" The doctor shook his head. "Nobody told me that, so I figured it was accidental." He walked to his bench, arranged some instruments and came back.

"Mean to tell me that somebody deliberately

torched that building and made damn sure that the only two doors out got set on fire first and both at the same time?"

"That's what witnesses I've talked to tell me, Doc."

"Be damned. I'm changing that death certificate to death by design by person or persons unknown. Means the case should be open."

"Just what I told the sheriff, and he didn't like it one bit. I'd guess he'll leave it open but won't do much."

The medic looked concerned for a moment. "Hell, I just went by what they told me. You're that federal lawman, I'd reckon. Heard you were in town." He took a step toward the door.

"Well, if there's nothing else . . ."

"No, that's all unless you tended another man for a gunshot wound this afternoon."

"You're my first, and I hope my only."

Spur eased out of the chair and went back to the street. His aches from this morning were still there, just muted a little. The doctor hadn't said a word about his face. Maybe he thought Spur always looked that way.

The newspaper tent was just ahead. He swung open the door and looked inside. Gypsy sat at her small desk working on a proof. She looked up when he came in and smiled.

"About time you got here. I have good news." She hurried to him and grabbed both his hands. "Really, really good news. Come out here."

In back of the tent they walked through a few stray beams to the spot where the press stood. The floor had burned through under it, and now the big press sat directly on the rocky ground. It was nearly level, and a young man in oil and greasy overalls worked on one of the levers.

"That's Mike from Phoenix. He's a whiz with presses. Says he can have mine up and running before dark. Isn't that wonderful!"

Spur enjoyed her enthusiasm. Her face lit up like an octogenarian's birthday cake, and her eyes sparkled.

"Good news, Gypsy. One more step in getting back to normal. Now you need that building and your printing supplies."

Her light mood vanished and she scowled. "Yes, both those things, and my bank account is starting to give out. It's my dowry money I've been spending. I could always sell the house. It's free and clear and should bring maybe twelve hundred dollars—furnished, of course."

"Don't sell the house. We'll figure out something. How about a small building first that you can expand later on? One just big enough for the press and some supplies, maybe twenty by forty feet set in the middle of the space here."

"Lumber, nails, roofing. I can't pay for a building that size."

"How about a basket social? All proceeds go to the new building for the *Clarion*. Make a basket and help the town get back the newspaper that it deserves."

Gypsy squinted slightly, thinking about it. She rubbed her chin, then looked up at him. "It just might work. I could print off some flyers and post them around town, then talk all the women I can see into making a basket. We'll have it Sunday afternoon in the park."

"Sounds good. Minimum bid two dollars. No limit on how high the bidding can go. Gypsy, your basket alone should fetch twenty dollars. Do you realize how many two by fours you can buy for a twenty dollar gold piece?"

"Yes, let's try it. I'll get the flyers set in type and proofed tonight, then print them off by lantern light. I could use some help if you're going to be around."

"Try to be."

She looked at him then stepped forward and touched his shoulder.

"That's a bandage around your arm. How did you hurt it?"

"A small disagreement with a man shooting a rifle. Nothing fatal."

"Oh, and your poor eye. I bet you didn't put any steak on that, did you?"

"Guilty, your honor."

"Your nose! I didn't even notice I was so excited about the press. Mike is charging me just for one day's work and the fare on the stage. Not even any new parts, he said. When the roof fell in it sagged away from the press before it dropped. Otherwise it could have ruined the whole machine." They walked back to her office area.

"Now, let me look at your nose. You sure you've seen a doctor about this?"

"Yes, I have. Don't mother me. I'm fine. You get to thinking about your box social. Talk it up with the women and get them to promise to come. If the married women all come their husbands will have to, and it'll work out fine."

"Oh, I hope so. I'm going to write the flyer right now and lay it out with some great big huge type. Wish we still had the circus wooden letters. Oh, well, we have some two inch." She waved and hurried off to work on the flyer.

Spur felt the pain boil up from his arm. The nerve endings had come out of their shock and now complained bitterly about being cut in half by that damn rifle slug.

He thought of going to the doctor for some pain killer, but usually the medics gave out laudanum. He'd come too close to getting addicted to that heroin derivative once. He wouldn't touch it now.

Instead he'd have a big supper at the fanciest eatery in town, then invent some games to take his mind off the pain and get to bed early. Sleep would be the best thing for him tonight.

By the time he walked to the Eagle's Nest Restaurant down near the end of Main, they were serving dinner. He had a fine meal of steak and pheasant, with all the trimmings and side dishes. It was delicious. The price was $1.75 and he nearly choked at the tab. How was he going to explain that meal on his expense account? He shrugged. They didn't believe half the things he claimed anyway.

He strolled the long way back to the hotel and arrived there slightly after eight o'clock. There were no notices in his key box, and he went directly to his room.

Spur went through his usual routine for opening the door, and this time when he pushed it in hard, he saw that two lamps were burning and Flo Benscoter sat on the bed smoking a long thin cigar.

He went in, closed the door and stared at her.

"I didn't know that you smoked cigars."

"I didn't either, until tonight. I got tired of waiting for you so I prowled around in your suitcase until I found your stogies. Flo, light the damned thing, I told myself. So I did. First few times I coughed and choked half to death, but by the time I got the second one smoked halfway down,

I got the knack of it. Not a bad tasting cheroot, old man."

"You're impossible."

"I know, McCoy. That's why you love to love me. I brought back the cheese and the wine."

"Good timing. I got shot today."

She jumped off the bed. "Poor darling. Who shot you? Where?"

"I don't know who, because he got away. The round went through my arm, so take it easy on my left one."

She pushed up his shirt-sleeve, kissed the white dressing and pulled him to the bed.

"You look like a man who needs some of my special brand of tender loving care. Just let Flo take care of everything. I know you're still hurting, but I won't make you hurt more. Not unless you bust a blood vessel when you come so hard. You just have your supper?"

He nodded.

"Good I slipped out for some sustenance as well." She unbuttoned his shirt and helped him ease the sleeve off his left arm, then pulled it away.

"Say now, I like manly chests, and yours is just fabulous. Enough hair and red nipples and muscles you haven't even used yet."

She knelt in front of him where he stood next to the bed. "Now, folks, we come to the good parts. Yeah, inside his pants. Want to see?" She opened his gunbelt buckle, took it off and hung it on the bedpost. She undid his belt and then his fly and in two more minutes had him stark naked and spread out on the bed like a sacrificial male virgin.

"Aye, that's more like it, laddie," Flo said.

"You're not Irish."

"And you're not English but you wear an English tweed."

She pulled off her clothes and eased down beside him.

"See how gentle I am so I don't hurt the poor warrior." She knelt beside him and lowered one breast to his face. "Hungry for a little dessert?" He chewed contentedly for a minute. Then she moved back and put her face close to his.

"Let's do something wicked and dangerous tonight, something wild and misguided, something absolutely wanton."

Spur put his hands under his head and let his gaze wash over her face and what of her naked body he could see without moving.

"What suggestions do you have?"

"I do have a young friend I share many things with. If you like I can go bring her in. She's seventeen, bright and nicely formed."

Spur shook his head. "I think one fine lady will be all I can handle tonight, even with the wine and cheese. Perhaps some other time."

"We could do it around the world. You ever done around the world before?"

Spur frowned. "Not that I know of. Explain."

"We pick out six countries, and then we make love in a fashion that's typical of that nation. We start with me on top for the first country, America. Then we go on to England and the proper missionary position. From there we bounce to France and we do it eating up one another."

Spur grinned. "I hope we get to Russia."

"That's next. You hit all three spots in one go round, and it's like a Russian bear. Then comes China, and we wind up in Mexico to the tunes of a mariachi band."

"We have to go in order?" Spur asked. His hands found her breasts and began caressing them, feeling the heat of them build and build.

"Hell, we can do them in any order you want to," she said, her breath coming in panting gulps now, her hands working on his erection, teasing him, stroking him.

"Stay on top," Spur said, and Flo gave a little cry of joy and moved down to position herself over his thrusting hips. She found the right place, held his erection straight up and eased down on him, his prick slashing upward into her slot until their pelvic bones ground together.

Flo let out a long low moan as they slid together. She kissed him and kept her mouth covering his as she lifted upward with her hips and dropped down on him. Her hips pounded against his, her mouth gasping for air as the whirlwind of her passion steamrolled over her, grinding her, shaking her body.

"Oh, my gawd!" Flo shouted. She gave one more powerful thrust of her slender hips and collapsed on top of him like a billowing tablecloth settling down on a rocky picnic spot.

She lay there panting. He figured she was nearly unconscious after her series of climaxes. He stirred, but she remained the same. He lifted one of her hands and let it go and it fell lifeless to the bed.

"My God, one fuck and she dies right on top of me," he said.

She giggled.

"Guess I'll have to get this ton of sexy flesh and bones and holes off me."

She rolled to the left of the bed. A moment later she sat up, worry clouding her face.

"My gawd, I didn't let you have your turn."

"Relax, I did mine while you were far out in space somewhere past our sun. How was your flight?"

"So good, you'll never know, because I can't describe it in mere words. I'd need an artist's pallet and a full stage of actors and musicians and dancers to show you how fine it was."

"What's left? Sounds like you experienced it all."

Flo shook her head. "No, no, no. Not all. I just can't wait for China's turn."

Spur had his hands clasped behind his head again. It gave him a strange sense of mastery. He didn't understand why. "China. You're waiting for China? We can't possibly get there until we hit France where we eat to our soul's content. Hey, naked lady, I sure as hell ain't gonna miss France."

Chapter Nine

Spur McCoy lay in his bed taking stock as the light at last turned dawn into day.

The lady had left sometime before.

His arm still hurt like fire and had awakened him.

His belly and chest felt better but still hurt with certain movements.

He was getting old, over 30 now.

Damn, what a night! He didn't care if he saw another naked lady for two or three days, at least.

They had tried to kill him twice now. He was stepping on some mighty big toes.

He wished he knew who the toes belonged to.

He had the name of Red Kenny to try to get some answers.

The initials on the note—J.F.—might be the real

thing or a fake. It was a possible second lead.

It was almost six A.M. and he should be getting up.

Spur McCoy summed it all up in a rush.

"Get your body out of bed, shaved, dressed and fed. Then see where Red Kenny lives and track the bastard down." He nodded. It sounded good saying it out loud.

It was nearly an hour later that he left the Home Café. Terri, the owner, had a big sign up about the basket social for the *Clarion*. Good. Now who would know where to find Red Kenny? The postmaster. He or she would know most everyone in town.

When he walked into the Benscoter General Store, he saw a new man behind the counter.

"Yes sir, what can we do for you today?"

"Is the postmaster around?"

"Mr. Ferris was called out of town. Just not sure when he's coming back. Mr. Benscoter made me the acting manager for the time being. That means I have to do the mail, too. Not a big job, but I like it."

The man speaking was not a day over 21 and had an open, honest face and what sounded like an ounce or two of common sense.

"Maybe you can answer my question. I'm looking for Red Kenny, big guy with red hair. You know where he works or where he lives?"

"Stayed at Ma Carlson's boarding house last I knew. Big Red is a man hard to miss. You might try Ma. She's the blue-trimmed white house a block up from the Pine Grove Bank on the corner of Main and Third."

"Obliged," Spur said and hiked out the door and down toward Third Street.

Ma Carlson shook her head. "Sorry, Red ain't

here. Was here up to yesterday, but he said he had a new job in Phoenix and had to get right down there. Gone lock, stock and britches."

"Well, reckon I won't talk to him any, that being the case. Thanks for your time."

He walked back to Main and leaned against the corner of a building and pondered his situation for a minute. Not a damn sight better than it had been when he woke up. Spur pushed away from the building, strolled up the street and into the *Clarion* tent. When Gypsy saw him she rushed up, threw her arms around him for a tight hug, then kissed his lips hard and fast and stepped back.

"Thank you, thank you, thank you! That idea about the basket social benefit is catching fire. Half the merchants have up signs and have stacks of flyers and are really getting behind the idea. I have you to thank for the whole thing."

"Well, another kiss and hug would be nice. That was so fast it didn't count."

Gypsy grinned. "I think you like this kissing stuff."

"I confess."

She reached up and without touching him kissed his lips with a light, gentle touch like a soft summer breeze. It stirred him more than anything had in a long time.

"Now the hug," he said with a hoarseness creeping into his voice. She put her arms around him, pushed her breasts firmly against his chest and lay her head on his shoulder. He guessed her eyes had closed. She held the hug longer than he thought she would, then she sighed and let go and stepped back. Her eyes glistened.

"So, that's part payment. I'm so excited about the box social I can hardly get any work done. Oh, you

didn't make it back last night to help on the flyers.
I hope you have a good excuse."

"I'll bring a note from my mother," he said, and
they both grinned.

"Mike left on the morning stage. The press is all
ready to go as soon as I get regular paper stock and
a five gallon can of ink."

"Where can you get that?"

"Mike said he'd ask the paper in Phoenix if they'll
lend me some paper and ink. I usually order it out
of a supply house in San Francisco. Takes about a
week to get here even on the train and stage."

"So another small paper this week?"

"Yes. Any progress on the fire?"

"Not much. I had a lead, but he suddenly left
town for a job in Phoenix."

"That sounds familiar. Papa used to say that
sometimes when he was chasing down a story."

"Right now I'm chasing in circles." Spur walked
back and forth in the confines of the tent and finally what had been digging away at the back of his
mind but never quite surfacing came out.

"Gypsy, did you father ever do any work at
home? Did he have a small desk there or a table
where he left things?"

"Yes, a small desk in the living room, a secretary
I think it's called. He said it was for home things,
not business."

"Sometimes the two get mixed up a little. Can we
take a look at it?"

"Right now or after dinner tonight? No, damn,
this is press day if I ever get this story finished. How
about right now?"

"Better than fine."

When they reached the house, she showed him
the desk in the living room. It had a swing down lid

that served as a writing table. Above were two glass doors in front of four shelves for knick knacks and below three drawers for storage.

"Papa told me he kept some records and important papers here."

"I'm hoping he left some of his notes or information about the big story he was working on."

"You take all the time you want. I haven't had a chance to go through it yet. I better get back to the paper."

"You're leaving a stranger alone in your house?"

She smiled and walked up to him slowly, letting her breasts sway and bounce as she came. "Hey, cowboy, you're not a stranger. I've kissed you twice, and you're a Secret Service man. How can I lose?"

"Maybe by getting kissed again."

"Deal!" she said and pressed against him and lifted her face for his kiss. Her eyes closed and she sighed and clung to him after the hot kiss ended.

"Oh, damn, McCoy, you turn my knees into jelly and make me feel so wonderful I don't want to leave your arms." She leaned back and looked at him. "Yes, I know a girl shouldn't tell a man he affects her that way. I'm new at this loving. Give me a little time to learn what to do and what not to do." She shook her head and stepped back. "Oh, damn," she said softly, then turned and ran out of the house.

He watched her go with a smile. Some little woman. She had aroused him in that short exchange. True, she should be more careful talking that way when she was in a man's arms.

He shook his head, sat down and began the job of going through the dead man's desk. He found some things that surprised him, but so far nothing that would give a clue about the big money swindle he was afraid was about to take place in town.

He had finished going through the drawers and had two more small pigeonholes to search when he came across a note scrawled on a piece of newsprint.

"Check county clerk for legal owners on commercial property." Below those words were these notes: "31 commercial properties. Owner of 17—Benscoter. Owner of 14 houses—Benscoter."

Spur stared at the notes. Why did Pinnick check out who owned what in town? He seemed only to be interested in which buildings and business firms Benscoter owned. Was that part of the Swindle or had something to do with it?

Spur didn't know but he saved the notes on the properties. Was it a waste of time? He wasn't sure and couldn't be until he had a meeting with Benscoter and evaluated the man himself.

"Oh, damn," he said softly the same way Gypsy had said earlier. He needed some kind of a break in this case. He was damned if he was going to let it beat him.

J. Lawton Benscoter glared at Loophole Larson who was sprawled in the chair on the other side of the cherry wood desk.

"What the hell do you mean Jessie wasn't on the morning stage to Phoenix? He's a walking dynamite bomb just looking for an excuse to go off. You saw what he said in that damned note. He was ready to sell us out for immunity. The little bastard would have dumped us right into prison to save his own neck. He's got to be out of town on the afternoon stage or else."

"J. Lawson, don't threaten me. I've been worked over by experts and they didn't find a chink in my armor. Look at it this way. I didn't just stop a prison sentence for you. I delivered into your hands a new partner—me."

Loophole stood, put his hands on the desk and glared down at the businessman. "Benscoter, I'm giving notice right now. I'm not risking prison for any damn ten percent. I know the sheriff is in, and that makes three of us. I want a third of the take. We split it three ways."

"Not a chance. The sheriff and I are the ones at risk. We could go up for a long time. You're just on the fringes of the conspiracy. Jury wouldn't hurt you much. This is foolishness. You advised us on the methods, we did the deed. Not acceptable at all. Forget it."

"Benscoter, you're forgetting something. I didn't send Jessie to Phoenix because I own him. He's mine. I can dust him off and take him to the district attorney any time I want to. I can telegraph the State Attorney General, tell him the situation and have you and Sheriff Willard behind bars in a day and a half."

"You threatening me?" Benscoter said, disbelief bursting out all over his face.

"Damn right. Either I get a third of the profits, or you and Willard go to prison. Take your choice."

Sweat seeped down Benscoter's balding head, running into his eyes. His face distorted, and he bellowed with rage.

"Damnit, Loophole, we had a deal, an agreement."

"On your terms. I did my work, now I want my fair share. I can get immunity from the attorney general by turning in you two. Jessie and I will both testify and you won't stand a chance. Take your choice."

Benscoter tried to calm himself. Storming into a bigger rage wouldn't help any. Loophole was tricky, sneaky. He knew that. This was the first time that it had been used against him. He tried to compose himself.

"Loophole, damnit, I hate this, but I can see your point. As a conspirator you stand to get the same sentence I would. You take the risk, you should get the benefits. All right. I agree. You get your share, one-third, after we pay off Jessie." Benscoter held out his sweaty hand. "Agreed?"

Loophole laughed, grabbed the hand and shook it. "Damn right, partner. How much do you think this should involve over the long run?"

"I'd say at least a hundred and fifty thousand dollars, more or less. That would mean fifty thousand for you."

Loophole laughed again. "Damn but that sounds good. At last I'm going to make some real money."

"Now, this brings up the problem of Jessie. Will it be enough to send him to Phoenix? What do you think, Loophole?"

"I been considering that. He tried to double-cross us by going to that Secret Service agent. He had the note written and was going to the hotel to deliver it when you caught him. Maybe we don't need him anymore."

"True, his part in the scheme is over. Friday morning it should all be completed and we'll be rich," Benscoter said.

"Then why not make sure he doesn't tell any-body—ever?"

Benscoter stared at Loophole. "You take care of that little task. You have him."

"Me? Hell, no. I don't do that kind of thing. Not a chance. I could hire somebody, but I wouldn't know where to look."

"You found the two riflemen to go after Spur McCoy on short notice."

"Lucky chance, J. Lawton. I'd rather leave this sort of thing up to you so it gets done right."

"Hell, Loophole, you're a full partner now. You should be doing your share of the work and take more risks." Benscoter stood, walked to the door and came back. He shook his head. "Hell, Loophole, I guess I can find somebody. I'll get it done. You bring Jessie here, up the back stairs. We can put him in that back room without any windows until it gets dark."

"Yeah, sounds good, J. Lawton. I'll go get him right now. Won't take fifteen minutes. Meet me at the head of the stairs."

"Disguise him somehow. A big hat or something. We don't want anybody happen to see him brought up those back stairs."

Loophole nodded. "I'll be back in fifteen minutes."

When the lawyer left, J. Lawton Benscoter scowled and wrote two names down on a pad—Jessie and Loophole. He drew a thick black line through Jessie's name and hesitated over the next one. He lay down the pencil.

Now he had to come up with a reliable man to do the job on Jessie. It would be better if no one ever found the body. One of the sinks or one of those little lakes to the north in the mountains. Yes, that sounded good. Some chain and some heavy rocks should do it for 20 years. By then he didn't care who found the skeleton.

J. Lawton took a deep breath. Yes, things were

moving along a little faster than he thought they might. Not exactly what he expected, but with a lawyer as smart as Loophole, he should have figured there would be complications.

He decided on the man he wanted. Plenty of time to notify him. He'd be at the Blue Goose, holding down the bar. Good man, but he drank a little. Hell, everyone drank a little.

Benscoter reached in the bottom drawer of his desk, took out a .45 derringer and slid it in his jacket pocket. It hardly showed. He liked to be armed now and then, especially when dealing with unpredictable men. He hadn't the slightest idea that Jessie would turn yellow on him. Damn. Now Loophole was kicking up his heels. Time would tell.

He heard a buggy coming round as he stood on the top of the back stairs up to his offices. Those back stairs sure had come in handy dozens of times.

When the rig pulled in Loophole got out, went to the other side and helped a man down. Benscoter couldn't tell who the man was. He appeared to be in pain. A large hat on his head shaded his face so Benscoter didn't recognize Jessie even though he knew it had to be him.

Loophole half-carried the smaller Jessie up the steps. Benscoter unlocked a room halfway along the corridor and all three went in. Benscoter lit a lamp on a small dresser. There was a single bed with mattress and blankets. A chamber pot showed under the bed. The room was ten feet square and had no windows and the one door.

Benscoter pulled the hat off Jessie Ferris's head. The man's hands were tried behind him. Benscoter backhanded him without warning, and

Jessie's head snapped to the left.

"Bastard!" Benscoter roared. "You tried to sell me out. If Loophole hadn't found you in time, we'd all be in jail by now. You damned fucking ingrate!" Benscoter's right fist slashed into Jessie's jaw, jolting him sideways. He stumbled and fell on the bed.

"Don't worry about screaming," Benscoter said, his breath coming fast, his face red from the fury. "You'll have a gag on soon enough.

Benscoter turned to Loophole. "Now that we have him here, are there any other traitors running around I don't know about?"

Loophole grinned and shook his head. "Hell, not a one. Just the three of us left. Sheriff ain't going nowhere, and neither am I. We just wait until Friday afternoon and start collecting."

Loophole paused. "Oh, you find the right man for the job?"

"I did," Benscoter said. "One I can trust and have trusted before, not one to see a chance to blackmail me and get away with a lot of my hard-earned cash."

Loophole frowned. "Hey, J. Lawton, you aren't insinuating that I was disloyal to you? Oh, God!"

J. Lawton Benscoter stood four feet from the lawyer who could see the derringer in the merchant's hand with the muzzle pointed directly at him.

"You really didn't think I'd let you blackmail me like this, did you, Loophole? You know me better than that. You got too big for your own good. Just because you can hoodwink and cheat and con these common folks around here is no reason to think you can do the same thing to me. I offered you a reasonable wage for your efforts.

You would have made fifteen thousand dollars. No, you wanted more."

"J. Lawton, I can't believe you're doing this. I'm your friend."

"I have no friends."

"I'm your lawyer. We've worked together for ten years."

"You've sponged off me for ten years."

Loophole began to sweat. Moisture popped out on his forehead and made little rivers down to his eyes and nose.

"What can I do, J. Lawton, to set this right? I'll go back to the ten percent. Fine. I can do that. I'll work for you for a year with no fee at all. Any legal work you need. Just don't leave me here."

"You don't have a chance in hell, Loophole. You betrayed me just as much as Jessie there did."

Loophole must have thought he saw a chance. He looked to the side, then when he must have thought Benscoter's eyes also turned that way, the tall lawyer charged the shorter, heavier man. The derringer fired. The round struck the lawyer in his belly. Loophole stumbled forward into Benscoter, his weight driving the smaller man back a foot. The muzzle of the small gun jammed into Loophole's chest.

Benscoter regained his balance and pulled the trigger again. The .45 caliber round smashed through a rib and rammed into the lawyer's heart, killing him in a second and a half.

J. Lawton Benscoter pushed the corpse away from him and let it fall to the floor. He turned the gun on the small man lying on the bed, his face white, his eyes wild with fear.

A moment later Jessie Ferris vomited on the floor, retching again and again.

J. Lawton Benscoter decided not to put a gag on the small man. It was nearing five o'clock. Everyone would have gone home soon. He had to get to the Blue Goose and tell his man he had a small job for him. Benscoter scowled and looked at the dead body on the floor. No, not one job—two jobs for him to do.

Chapter Ten

Spur McCoy walked the dusty streets of Pine Grove wondering what he should do next. He had to see J. Lawton Benscoter sooner or later to set his mind at ease. He should stop by at the courthouse and inquire of the county clerk about who owned certain properties in town.

He also had a commitment to help Gypsy run off the paper tonight on the proof press. He didn't even want to think how many times he would have to push that heavy roller back and forth to create the small newspapers. Only four pages tonight she said, so that was four times the number of issues— 200? Already his arms hurt.

He settled for the courthouse and found the county clerk's office.

The clerk's office was filled with large volumes of records that held a detailed account on every piece of property in the county that had been bought, sold, a lien filed against or any legal action taken against. It listed chapter and verse on all of them.

The county clerk was a heavy-set man with a forward jutting chin and small black eyes not wide enough apart. His brows grew together in the middle, and his black hair licked at his forehead as if trying to take over new territory.

"You want to know what?"

"Wondered how many pieces of property are owned in the county by J. Lawton Benscoter."

"You a reporter or something?"

"No, just interested."

"Oh, yeah, now I got it. You're that government lawman who's been nosing around. Don't have to look up the legals on Benscoter. Fact is the paper's publisher—ex-publisher I figure I should say—came in two weeks ago asking the same question. He put in about two days going over the volumes. Came up with seventeen business firms and fourteen houses."

"That seems like a lot," Spur said.

"I don't judge, just keep the books all legal and square and in order like I'm supposed to. Used to be a county clerk back in Illinois. Not much different here, just fewer people and fewer pieces of property. Most of it is still federal land. Lots will go to the state if and when we ever get enough people to qualify."

"How many does it take?"

"Sixty thousand souls in the state, and got to have all regular elected officials. Hell, we got the counties and officers. All we need is more people."

"Any idea how Benscoter got all these properties?"

"Ain't my job to know. I just record the transactions." The clerk looked up, squinting one eye. "Official or unofficial?"

"Oh, unofficial, by all means."

"Some folks say he cheated a few out of their houses. He runs the bank, too, you know. Then he foreclosed on a couple of business firms that didn't quite make a go of it. All legal and proper, just in a shitty way on some of them. Couple of months overdue on payments and—Wham, he forecloses."

The clerk closed one of the big books that held the records.

"Anything else I can do for you?"

"Can't think of a thing."

"See you spending time with that sweet little Gypsy. You planning on needing a marriage license, I issue them here."

"Not in my plans, but thanks."

Spur grinned as he left the courthouse and stopped by the sheriff's office. A deputy said the sheriff was gone for the day and would be in about ten the next morning.

It was five o'clock. Spur headed for the Benscoter building, went up to the second story and pushed open the unlocked door of the office of Benson Properties.

Alice had just finished clearing her desk for the day. She looked up and smiled. "Yes, sir, what can I do for you?"

"I'd like to see Mr. Benscoter. Is he in?"

"I believe he's still here. Just a moment. Who should I say is calling?"

"Spur McCoy."

She nodded and went through the door marked private after a quick knock. Spur could not hear any conversation through the door. He looked around the reception area and saw two chairs, a soft couch, a vase with some nearly wilted flowers and two framed prints on the walls. The place had touches of quality.

Alice came out the door and nodded. "Mr. Benscoter will see you, Mr. McCoy, but he has only five minutes. There's a meeting he has to get to. this way, please."

He went into the office. It had a carpet on the floor, curtains at the large windows, a sofa at one side with several pillows and a large desk and leather chair. Benscoter stood behind the desk but didn't offer to shake hands.

"Yes, Spur McCoy. I've heard you were in town. You're some kind of a federal lawman?"

"Yes, Mr. Benscoter, I'm with the Secret Service. We're empowered with jurisdiction in every state and territory as well as the unimproved lands across the West."

"What can I do for you?"

Plenty, Spur thought, if you only would. "I'm interested in the death of Andrew Pinnick. I've encouraged the sheriff to reopen the case since it is reported that coal oil was used to start fires at both the front and back doors of the newspaper office at the same time, trapping Pinnick inside. That's murder. Denying Pinnick his ability to exercise his freedom of the press rights is violating his civil rights, also a felony and a federal crime. I'm wondering what you've heard about the case."

Not a flicker of an eyelash, no intake of breath, no nervous hand movements. Either Benscoter had nothing to hide or was a master at controlling himself.

"Pinnick, yes, he's been here a while. He and I never saw eye to eye on everything, but he did put out a good paper. He was concerned about the city, about our people. A lot of things we did agree on, like when the railroad built as far as Phoenix and stopped. They had grade surveys all the way to Flag, but claimed it was too expensive to build and their land grants from the government for putting down the rails weren't big enough for this tough mountainous country. We both fought them on that a few years ago, and we lost."

Spur waved one hand to get Benscoter's attention. "I'd say you both were on a tough nut on that issue. Any reason you can think of why somebody would kill Pinnick?"

"Been doing some thinking on that. He was a prominent man in town. I'm a bit of a prominent man as well. Wondering if somebody has his sights on me. Not that I worry about it. Just a thought."

Spur had made up his mind and stood up. "Well, I better be moving on. Have a few more people to talk to. Good to meet you." Spur didn't offer to shake hands and neither did Benscoter.

Outside, Spur walked down the steps to Main and wandered down the boardwalk. He came to a place where there was a vacant lot for someone to build on. Since there was no store there, there was no boardwalk in front of the lot. Each store owner put up his own boardwalk out front. On hills the boardwalks sometimes mismatched and were not level.

Here, Spur stepped down to the dirt, went across it and up to the boardwalk on the other side in front of the bank. Benscoter owned that, too.

His impression of the town's richest man was not favorable. The man was a talker, a salesman of the first order, and with that gift of gab, he could sell a lot of things that shouldn't be sold.

Spur simply didn't trust the man. He had a feeling in his gut that he was looking at an enemy, but he had no proof what-so-ever. He wasn't afraid of Benscoter, but he knew he was a man to watch.

Spur turned and walked back to the Pine Grove Hotel, slipped into the dining room and had the specialty of the day, elk steak with a special sauce. The elk was cooked exactly right, not over-done. It was the best elk steak he had eaten in years. Somebody had bled the big animal soon after killing it to keep the blood from seeping into the meat.

He had some of the newfangled ice cream sprinkled with fresh strawberries. By the time he got to his room he was ready for a quick nap before he decided what to do for the evening.

Just as he put his key in his door, Flo came out of a room down the hall and waved at him. He closed his eyes. Not tonight, he implored. He wasn't in that good of shape.

Flo timed it perfectly. She walked toward him, and the minute he stepped into his room, she slid in after him and closed the door.

"I've missed you," she said.

"How could you? It's only been about ten hours."

"Hours and minutes mean little to me. I live for the moment."

"Good. Tell me about your husband. I just met him and had a short, unsweet talk. He's rich, I know, but what does he do all day to take up his time?"

"Plans how he can get richer."

"Does he ever talk about his plans?"

"We don't talk a lot. Now and then he tries out an idea on me to see how I react."

"What kind of ideas?"

"Moneymaking schemes. Once he had a mortgage on the hardware store. He wanted the store, since it was making money. He started a whispering campaign that the owner had been a rebel captain during the war in charge of a prison camp where a lot of Yanks died. The man's business fell off. Then he spread rumors about the man's wife, said she slept around. The man was furious. His business suffered. J. Lawton came up with one little plan after another to harass the man, and he got so worried and confused that he forgot to make a mortgage payment. J. Lawton pounced, and the next day he foreclosed on the note. The man couldn't pay up, so J. Lawton took the business and has been running it ever since."

"Your husband sounds like a real winner."

"He is, if you like money. I do. I like money and what it can buy, and I like a man hot and sweating, pumping away on top of me. Why are you looking at me that way?"

"Because I'm too tired and too sore and my arm hurts too much where I was shot. Which means no sex tonight."

"Oh, fuck!"

"Figured you'd be understanding about my condition."

"So what do you want to do tonight?"

"We could search your husband's office."

"Yeah?"

"You could help get me inside and we could see what kind of dirty tricks he's working up. Does he spend much time in his office at night?"

"Not usually. He puts in time at the Blue Goose, his saloon. He plays cards in the back room and plays with a fucking whore's tits when he isn't at the card table."

"Do you want to?"

"Want to make love right now? Fuck, yes."

"No, do you want to help me search his office?"

"Oh." She shrugged. "I guess so. Might be exciting. I've never done any burglary before. We going to steal money from his safe?"

"No, just look through the place. I think something big is about to happen in Pine Grove. I think your husband is behind it or has a hand in it. Something must be written down."

Flo stood and opened her blouse, letting her breasts swing out, and then walked up to Spur. "Kiss my girls a little first, just to make them feel better. They figured on a wild fucking time tonight."

He bent and kissed them, then nibbled at the brown nipples until she squealed.

"Oh, yeah, my girls like that. Now, you want to break in or use my key to the back door?"

They stood in deep shadows 50 feet from the back stairs of the Benscoter building. When first they came up the alley they had seen a buggy leaving.

"Did that rig leave from your husband's building?" Spur asked.

"I didn't see it any better than you did. Nobody's around now if they did come from there. No lights on front or back. Let's go up there and play."

They walked the rest of the way through the alley and went up the back steps as if they belonged there. Flo dug a key out of her reticule, and Spur opened the back door. When they stepped inside Spur touched her shoulder to keep her still as he listened.

He heard nothing. "Where's his office? Toward the front?" She nodded and led the way down a short hall to a door. She pushed it open. Inside the room had only one window that faced the side of a two story building three feet away.

"Nobody from the street could see a light in here," Flo said. "What are you hunting for?"

"I don't know. When I find it, I'll let you hear."

Spur struck a match, found a lamp and lit it, then turned it down low. He put it on the big desk and pulled out drawers looking for files, papers, notes, anything. He found a bottle of Scotch whiskey, a derringer that had recently been fired, and a lot of papers, cards and envelopes.

On top of the desk sat a small square cardboard box three inches deep. In it were papers and two pencils. Some of the papers were fastened together with a straight pin pushed through two places.

One was a contract to buy a piece of property west of town. Another was an agreement to furnish water from a runoff stream to a farmer's small acreage. Spur sat in the big chair behind the desk and shook his head. He had no idea what he was hunting.

"I'll be damned. Look at this," Flo said. She brought it over closer to the light. It was a small poster like one Spur had seen in San Francisco's Chinatown. It showed 116 different sexual positions featuring well-endowed oriental men and women.

"J. Lawton, you old dog. We'll just have to try some of these. Damn, wish I could keep this. He'd miss it. Maybe I can take it now and bring it back later. Yes!"

Spur made one more look, this time through some files in a long box. He found documents about houses and buildings and businesses, but that was about it. He was just ready to turn out the lamp and give up when he saw an envelope sticking out from under a blotter on the big desk. He pulled it out and looked at it.

In the upper left-hand corner was the return address. It was county stationery. The hand-written name on the envelope was not that of Benscoter. Stamped on the envelope was an official post office mark that read "Registered". In an empty box was a handwritten number in ink.

What was a registered letter to Amos K. Rondell doing in Benscoter's office, mostly hidden under a blotter? He noticed that the end of the envelope had been cut off.

Gently, Spur shook out the letter inside, and he and Flo both read it.

It was handwritten on county letterhead. It said: "Mr. Amos K. Rondell, this is your third notice that your property is in default on county taxes. If your arrears bill is not paid in full by Friday, June 23, the county will take appropriate legal action."

There was a the legal description of the property, and the statement that he owed $146 in back taxes. Then the letter was signed by the county treasurer.

"This mean anything to you?" Flo said.

Spur frowned. Something seemed to register far back in his mind, but it slipped away. He wrote down the name and address and the amount of the tax and the registered number, then put the letter in the envelope and the envelope back under the blotter.

"Let's get out of here. I just struck out again. One of these damn days I'm going to have to hit a homerun or I'll get thrown off the team."

"You're still at bat on my team," Flo said trying to rub his crotch. He leaned away from her.

"Maybe tomorrow. I told you I'm plumb fucked out for today."

"Damn, Spur, you ain't no fun no more."

"Woman, when a body hurts, it just isn't fun."

They slipped out the back door of the office, made sure the door was locked and went down the rear steps.

At the bottom, they went down the alley where Flo pulled Spur to a stop and kissed him.

"Spur, violating J. Lawton's office just made me all sexy as hell. How about a quick one, standing up, right here? Nobody ever comes through this alley. Hey, you ever fucked in public this way before? A real kick, a wild thrill. Makes me shiver just thinking about it. Come on, spoil-sport, just a quick one right here, right now."

She backed against the wall of a building in the shadows. Flo lifted her long skirt and bunched it around her waist. She caught his hand and pulled him over to her.

Flo put his hand to her crotch. Spur laughed softly. "You ain't wearing a damn thing under your dress."

"So, take advantage of the chance, right now. Might not happen like this ever again."

Spur McCoy was suddenly so sexually excited he could hardly keep from shivering. He ripped open the buttons on his fly and pulled out his penis. He had a full erection. Flo giggled, then leaned against the wall, laced her fingers together behind his neck, jumped up and fastened her legs around his back.

"You've done it this way before," Spur said.

"Once or twice, but never outside in public. Come on, Spur, right now, fuck me hard."

It was an offering that Spur could not turn down.

Chapter Eleven

Spur McCoy and Flo left the alley laughing softly and feeling like teenage kids who did something naughty in public.

"That was a first for me," Spur said. He studied the woman beside him who so recently had been one driving, grinding mass of sexual excitement.

"I'm not in the habit of copulating in public places either. What a hoot!"

"Oh, damn!" Spur said.

"What, what?"

"I forgot I had an appointment tonight. Sorry I have to just fuck and run, but it's important."

"Hell, I got the best part of you. Run along. Maybe we'll get together again, like tomorrow."

"Maybe. I have to go." He turned and hurried up Main Street. He saw Flo sticking to the shadows as she walked in the opposite direction. He real-

ized he had no idea where she lived, where the
Benscoter house was.

He forgot about that when he saw the lights on
in the *Clarion* tent ahead. He looked inside, but saw
no one. Around the side of the tent he saw three
lamps where the proof press had been positioned
in the center of the burned-out newspaper office.

There he saw Gypsy rolling the heavy proof
press cylinder. He walked back, calling out from
the darkness to let her know he was coming.

"Hello, there. I'm late." He walked into the light.
She had a smudge of ink on her nose, another on
her right cheek. She blew a stand of her long hair
out of her eyes and frowned at him.

"You are extremely late, but then so am I. I
haven't even finished the first page yet. You're
welcome to help, if you want to."

"Why I came."

He watched her put the sheet of paper over the
inked type, roll the cylinder across it, peel off the
printed page and put it on a box to one side.

"That's all there is to it. If you can do the rolling,
I'll put on the sheets and take them off and ink the
roller. It'll go faster that way."

Again he compared this sweet young girl to Flo.
Their ages weren't all that much different, but the
different quality was something to see. Gypsy wore
a smock over her dress, but it didn't conceal her
good breasts and tight little waist.

"Think you can manage this?"

"I think so. Just make sure I don't flatten your
hand against the type."

"Not a chance. I'm faster than that."

They began to print the pages which soon came
down to a rhythm, and in five minutes they had finished the first page.

"I'm only doing two hundred copies," Gypsy said. "We won't have time for much more than that. Anyway I'm running out of the small paper. I mooched paper from everyone I knew. Tomorrow I'm going down to Phoenix to try to get some larger paper and a can of ink."

He put the second page on the proof press, and they started the job again. Halfway through she looked up.

"You hear the latest news? Loophole Larson, our town's best lawyer, got himself killed tonight. Evidently it was a brawl in back of a saloon. The barkeep at the Blue Goose said he heard some wild yelling and shots, and by the time he got into the alley, Loophole had two holes in him, one through his heart."

"Is Larson important to help us find the arsonists?"

"He could be. Larson was Benscoter's lawyer. He'd worked with Benscoter on several questionable deals. Papa said he knew something wasn't right with them, but they were legal and there was nothing he could do. Maybe a falling out of thieves?"

"Maybe. But why a back alley brawl? Doesn't quite sound in character for this Larson."

"Not at all in character. But if you've got a body on your hands it makes a good cover-up." Gypsy missed placing the page straight on the type, and he stopped the roll. "Another interesting fact is that Benscoter owns the Blue Goose and can tell his barkeep what to say and what to tell the sheriff."

Spur talked as he rolled the cylinder, printing page two on the back of page one.

"This is starting to pile up evidence against

Benscoter. It must mean we have the wrong man. He's the richest man in town. Someone who does handyman work for him and who hired two shooters to put lead in my body suddenly leaves town. A dead man turns up in back of a saloon he owns, and the barkeep swears he had been inside moments before and went out back to settle an argument or some such.

"Just too much of it. He's either in the wrong place at the wrong time or guilty as hell. Hey, what would you think if I told you I prowled Benscoter's office tonight and found a registered letter addressed to someone else half-hidden on Benscoter's desk?"

"You broke into his office?"

"Not exactly. I used a key. The whole thing wasn't lawful, but nobody is watching me. What about a registered letter?"

"Might have been delivered and the person it was sent to showed it to Benscoter for some reason."

"True, might be. Wouldn't hurt to ask the man it was sent to if he ever got it. Just a hunch I have."

"You always play your hunches?"

"Usually."

"Well, I have a hunch side two is done. Now on to page three."

They finished printing about ten o'clock, then collated the two pages and folded them in half so they would stay together.

"You going to help me deliver them?" Gypsy asked, her eyes sparkling.

"Now? In the middle of the night?"

"Best time, then the subscribers have the paper bright and early in the morning."

"Who gets the papers?"

"Every store and every house as far out as we want to walk."

"No subscribers?"

"Some, but we need the circulation to charge for the advertising. You don't know much about running a newspaper, do you?"

They finished delivering the last of the papers about one A.M. They had covered every door in the town. He walked her back to her porch and collapsed on the front steps.

Gypsy sat down beside him.

"Nice night?"

"Tired night. I'd be more at home delivering those papers on horseback."

"The cowboy who never walks when he can ride his horse. You're not really a cowboy."

"Did a trail drive once, about a hundred miles. Enough to make me know I didn't want to do it again."

"What now?"

"Oh, something you might know. I got a note from somebody with the signature of J.F. You know anybody in town with those initials?"

"Mmmm, let me think. F. That could be Feldon, Franklin or Fife. No, wrong first names. Ferris, hey, Jessie Ferris, the postmaster. That's his initials."

"The postmaster. Jessie Ferris went to visit his mother. Isn't in strange how everyone I want to talk to is out of town.

"Or dead. Loophole Larson, for instance."

He stood. "My next visit is going to be to the man who was supposed to have received the registered letter. I've got his name here somewhere." He found the scrap of paper.

"Amos K. Rondell. That name mean anything to you?"

"No, not at the moment. There is a family of Rondells here. I went to school with one of the girls, I think. Yes, they own a little ranch not far out of town. A homestead. Mr. Rondell wasn't much of a farmer but he did prove up on it."

"I'm going to go see Mr. Rondell first thing in the morning. Which direction out of town?"

"South."

When he stood and helped her up, she pushed up close to him.

"Time we get to bed," he said. "In separate beds," he added quickly.

She nodded, leaned in and put her arms around him. He bent and kissed her upturned face. A polite kiss. She made a growling sound in her throat, and he kissed her again like a lover. She sighed when they broke apart.

She looked at him a moment, then put her head on his shoulder.

"That was more like it. Sometimes I dream about you, Spur McCoy. Sometimes. But not tonight, I'm too tired."

She reached up, brushed her lips across his, stepped into her house and closed the door.

The next morning, Spur rented a horse, got directions to Amos K. Rondell's small ranch and rode out. The fresh green of the pines invigorated him. He loved the open country. Two grouse kicked out of some brush and took off with a furious flapping of wings. He trained an imaginary shotgun at them and fired. He would have nailed the second one.

The ranch house was little more than a one room cabin with a lean-to on the back. No barn, no corral. He found a one row walking plow and a fenced pasture for three cows and a pair of young steers. Meat and milk. A big garden was next to a small stream that wound its way down the slope.

A big dog barked a greeting as Spur stepped down from his mount. The screen door slammed and a man in overalls and a faded wide-brimmed hat came out of the side door. He carried a rifle over one arm, aimed at the ground.

"Morning," Spur said. "Mr. Rondell?"

"The same. Who you be?"

"Name's Spur McCoy. I'm a federal lawman. I need to ask you a few questions if you've got a moment."

"Got all day. Mind sitting outside here?"

Spur said he didn't, and they sat on a log across a sawhorse.

"Hear your homestead is all proved up," Spur said.

"About the size of it."

Rondell was a man with arms and legs that didn't seem attached right. He was loose-limbed and lean with a full beard in need of trimming. His hair had been long, Spur guessed, but now had been chopped off around the back to collar length.

"What about taxes, Mr. Rondell, your county taxes? Have you been paying them every year?"

"Taxes? Don't understand much about that. Figure I done my bit by proving up the land and it's mine. Don't need to pay nobody for owning it."

"There are county land taxes, Mr. Rondell. That's how the county raises enough money to hire a sheriff and county recorder and the essentials of county government."

"Don't vote for none of them, so don't reckon I got to pay taxes to them."

Spur nodded. Just what he had been afraid of. "Mr. Rondell, what I'm going to ask you is extremely important. Think about your answer before you tell me. Have you received in the mail in the last two or three weeks a letter from the county that was registered? That means you have to sign your name for the letter on a slip of paper at the post office. Did you sign for and pick up a letter like that lately?"

"Nosiree. Even if one of them registered ones come, I don't collect it. Don't take any mail with the county's name on it. Nope, don't believe in no county."

"You're sure you didn't sign your name on a receipt for a registered letter from the county?"

"Damn sure, son. Told you once. Don't like to chew my cud twice."

"Then nobody has told you that you owe the county a hundred and forty-six dollars in back taxes."

"No sir. Don't pay taxes. Ain't right."

Spur nodded. "Seems like a man should own what he owns, but that isn't always the case. Do you know that if you don't pay the taxes, the county sheriff can sell your homestead, land, house, the whole thing? Sell it to the highest bidder over a hundred and forty-six dollars?"

"Nope, don't know that. Anybody tries to move in or move me off got about three rifles and two shotguns aimed right down their gut to stop them."

"I'm sorry about this, Mr. Rondell, but it's the way our laws are written. I just wanted to find out if you received the letter or not. There's some skullduggery going on in town, and I'm trying to put a stop to it."

"Good, but I'm still not paying any damn taxes.

My land, I proved it up. The United States government said I own it. Got me the paper in the house there."

Spur stood and nodded. "I'm due back in town. Somebody will be out to talk to you about the taxes again. Don't shoot them. Talk with them. Make some payments and do it all in time. Otherwise you could lose your 'stead here."

Spur waved and stepped into his saddle. So the registered letter was never delivered. Were they mailed? As he rode back he knew that one was mailed—Rondell's. It had a stamp on it and a hand canceled postmark. Were other letters sent? The county treasurer was the man to ask.

Spur couldn't wait to get back to the courthouse to ask the treasurer about it.

A little over an hour later, county treasurer Paul Sedgwick nodded. "Absolutely, Mr. McCoy. I addressed about half of those letters myself. I personally selected the forty-seven county citizens who were at least two years in arrears on their tax payments and sent them letters showing the amount. The letter also warned them that appropriate legal action would be taken if they did not respond within fifteen days. I send out letters like this every year. Strange this year, though. Not a single one of those forty-seven has responded. Seems damn strange now that I think of it."

"Did you mail a letter to Amos K. Rondell?"

Treasurer Sedgwick chuckled. "You know our man Amos? Yes, he got a letter. Every two or three years I go out and reason with him. He at last gives in and sends us a beef or some hogs or some grain that we can turn into cash and apply against his taxes. He just doesn't understand about how taxation works."

"All right, I'm getting myself oriented here, Mr. Sedgwick. Now what happens if these forty-seven don't respond by the deadline?"

"Simple. I can turn them over to the county sheriff and instruct him to conduct a sheriff's sale of the properties in question at no less an amount than the taxes owed. Usually this is done with an auction, with the owner of the property free to make a bid. Often a man buys back his own property for the cost of the taxes."

"But anyone can bid?"

"Oh, absolutely. Sometimes I'll hold a property off the sale if the owner in good faith says he's trying to pay or makes a partial payment. We have a certain amount of leeway here."

"You notify the owners by registered mail. Isn't there more to it than that?"

"You bet. Three weeks before the sheriff's sale, the properties have to be listed in an advertisement in the official county newspaper, notifying all property owners that they are behind in their taxes and that a sale will be held if they don't respond."

"Did you place the ad?"

"Oh, yes, right on schedule. In fact I'd say we had it in and the proof approved three days before the paper's deadline."

"Mr. Sedgwick, do you have a copy of the printed advertisement? Isn't that a part of the permanent records you must keep?"

"Yes, indeed. I'm sure it's in the file. Let me take a look." The treasurer went to a wooden filing cabinet and leafed through some folders. He frowned and checked again. When he came back he had a folder with the date on top and opened it.

"Here's the folder with the selected taxpayers

who are in arrears. Also I have a copy of the letter that went out and the date. But nowhere do I find a copy of the advertisement."

"What was the date the ad was supposed to run in the paper?"

"Let's see, it should be here. Yes, it was to run on May 25th."

"I'm not sure, Mr. Sedgwick, but wasn't that just two days after the fire at the *Clarion?* I don't think your ad ever ran. The ad and the copy and the whole paper burned up on May 23rd and killed Mr. Pinnick."

Sedgwick looked at a calendar and scowled. "Damn, you're right."

"Then, Mr. Sedgwick, any sheriff's sale wouldn't be legal, would it? The proper procedure for advertising the indebtedness was not carried out."

Paul Sedgwick's eyes went wide. "But I already certified the properties, all forty-seven of them. They are to be put up for auction this afternoon at four P.M. on the front steps of the courthouse."

"You've got to stop it, Sedgwick. Amos Rondell swears he never received any registered letter from you. I saw the envelope with a postmark on it and your letter inside it on the desk of J. Lawton Benscoter last night. The only way it could have been there is for the postmaster to have stopped delivery on those registered letters. I think he did that and then destroyed the letters. In effect, none of the forty-seven property owners on that list were notified of this sheriff's sale in either of the two ways the law specifies that they must be notified."

"But I can't stop the auction. Once I've certified them to the sheriff, it's out of my hands. Only the sheriff can call it off once things have gone this far."

Spur grabbed the treasurer by the arm. "Come on, Sedgwick. You and I are going to go have a serious talk with Sheriff Ben Willard. It eleven o'clock already. We don't have much time."

Chapter Twelve

The county treasurer and Spur McCoy rushed down the corridor to the other side of the courthouse where the sheriff's offices were. A lethargic deputy looked up at them when they raced into the room.

"Got to see the sheriff," Sedgwick snapped.

"Sheriff?"

"Yes, Sheriff Willard. Is he here?"

"Oh, the sheriff. Nope, he's not in right now."

"Where did he go?" Spur asked.

"Don't rightly know. Said he'd be back about four o'clock this afternoon. Might try the Blue Goose."

Spur talked quietly with Sedgwick. "He's holed up somewhere until the sale. He's planned it this way. No chance to stop the sale if we can't find him."

"Let's check the Blue Goose," Sedgwick said.

They were halfway there when Spur saw a horse being led down Main Street. The man and horse had a string of six or eight boys chasing after him and pointing. Something had been slung over the back of the horse.

They stopped to watch and soon realized that the horse carried a body, head down, over the saddle.

"Not another body," Spur said. He and the treasurer went out to check. Sedgwick lifted the man's head and grunted.

"Yep, know him. Jessie Ferris, our late postmaster. He must be the one who stopped my registered letters. He must have signed for them as well, forging all of those signatures. If he was in on the conspiracy, somebody made sure he won't talk about it."

"Benscoter. It has to be Benscoter. How does he profit from all of this?"

Sedgwick explained it. "Simple. They have the auction, but nobody knows about it. One man shows up and makes a bid for one dollar over the amount of the tax on each property. The bidder picks up property, buildings, ranches, houses at a tenth or a fiftieth of their value. A lot of folks will protest if this happens. Then all the facts would come out. The lawyers would argue that there was an honest attempt to comply with the law, but the newspaper burned down. Somehow the letters that were mailed in good faith never got delivered. Then the lawyers would argue the case for months, maybe years in the courts. So we have to stop the sheriff somehow before it gets that far."

"Can you give me a list of those property owners, all forty-seven of them, who face the sheriff's sale?

"Why?"

"We need to have them at that auction if it takes place. Then at least they can buy their property back. Exposing the secrecy of the plan just might be enough to topple it. But we have to contact those property owners."

Sedgwick turned around. "Let's go back to the courthouse. Take about ten minutes to get the list together with their addresses. Then I'll go hunting the sheriff."

"You think the sheriff is in on the scheme?"

"He has to be or it wouldn't work."

"All right. You get me that list. I need to send a telegram. Meet you there."

Spur ran to the telegraph office a block down from the courthouse. He sent the wire to the Arizona Territorial Attorney General, in Phoenix.

"Sir. Complete law and order breakdown in Pine Grove. Sheriff Ben Willard engaged in gigantic fraud to hold auction of property for taxes without notifying property owners. Request you send deputy attorney general to take over Sheriff's duties until a new one can be appointed." He signed it Spur McCoy, United States Secret Service Agent, number 0041.

The clerk read it and scowled. "Is this true?"

"Damn right. You know anybody who's delinquent in his property taxes, you better have them get right over to the county courthouse."

Spur paid for the wire and ran back to the courthouse. Sedgwick had the list ready with businesses in one group and homes and ranches in another.

Spur ran to the newspaper and briefed Gypsy. "We've got to notify these people as quickly as we can. You take half the businesses and I'll take the other half, then we'll see if we can find the houses."

"So that's the conspiracy. They burned down the paper so we couldn't publish that list of threatened properties. It was a long list. I prepared the ad, but forgot all about it with the paper burning—and all."

"Right. Now we've got to rush. You ready?"

"Yes, absolutely. We've got to stop this scheme before it ruins those forty-seven families."

They hurried toward the first stores on their list. There were six for each to contact.

Spur talked to the saddle maker and leather shop owner.

"Hell, nobody contacted me. Ain't they supposed to send a registered letter? Did last year."

Spur told the man to be at the courthouse by two o'clock and hurried on to the next one. It was almost an hour later before Spur and Gypsy met back at the newspaper tent.

"Now what about the houses?" Gypsy asked. They divided them so they each had half the town.

"Have the people be at the courthouse at two o'clock," Spur instructed.

It was nearly one o'clock before they both returned to the newspaper.

Spur grinned and kissed her cheek. "Hey, thought you said you were going to Phoenix today to get newsprint."

"I was, but I overslept and missed the stage."

"Good. This is going to be the biggest story of the year. You know somebody found Jessie Ferris shot to death."

"I heard. He must have been the weak link. He must have been the one who wrote that J.F. note asking you to meet him to tell you about the conspiracy."

"So now we have the conspirators for murder as well—Jessie and probably Loophole Larson."

"Then Loophole would have been in on it to steer them around any legal problems," Gypsy said.

"Looks like it. He might have told them by burning down the newspaper they could prove that they tried to have the advertisements run. Then they could claim mailing the letters, since the treasurer did that and would testify accordingly. They just might convince the court the legal requirements had been met. The postmaster was a vital element in the conspiracy."

"Let's get over to the courthouse."

As they walked that way they saw little groups of people and noticed that several of the men had rifles and shotguns. He didn't want this to turn into a mob.

By the time they got to the courthouse, there were 20 people on the steps waiting. The treasurer, Sedgwick, was there talking to the people quietly.

Sedgwick saw Spur and told him he couldn't find the sheriff. "He's hiding out somewhere, waiting to come at the last minute to hold the auction."

"I doubt if the people here will let him do that," Spur said. "We don't want a mob, but I'm not sure we can stop it if it starts to get out of hand. A lot of these people are furious at the underhanded scheme the sheriff tried to pull. They don't know anything about Benscoter, but since he had that registered letter, he has to be one of the main partners."

"Think he'll come and do the bidding?" Gypsy asked.

"Not a chance," Spur said. "He'll send one of his clerks or a dummy of some kind to do his bidding."

The crowd increased in size.

"Where's the sheriff?" somebody bellowed.

"Let's string up the bastard!" another voice screamed.

Spur went to the top of the steps and fired his six-gun twice in the air. That quieted the crowd.

"Listen to me, you people," Spur thundered. By then there were about 100 people milling around the front of the court house. "My name is Spur McCoy. I've met a lot of you. I'm a United States lawman. I work with the Secret Service directly under the president. I came here to get this situation straightened out."

"Then let's do it by hanging the crooked damn sheriff," somebody in the crowd shouted.

"That's exactly what we won't be doing," Spur bellowed. "Two wrongs won't set things right. What we have to do is to stop the sheriff's sale—and do it legally. Then everyone wins. Now settle down, put your guns away, and let's get this done properly. First I have a couple of questions. Was anyone here notified about being delinquent in your taxes in the last two or three weeks by registered letter, the kind you have to sign for to get from the post office? Anybody?"

Not a person raised a hand or called out.

"All right, that's important, because by law, the treasurer must notify you before a sheriff's sale can be held. The treasurer will swear that he mailed the letters at the post office. We believe that the postmaster, Jessie Ferris, who was just found today shot dead, received those letters and then collected them and burned them so they couldn't be delivered."

There were some shouts in the crowd. One man bellowed out clearly. "Good riddance then to the bastard."

"We think the conspirators shot Jessie to keep him quiet. He tried to come forward and tell me about the swindle, but they caught him and killed him. Secrecy about the sheriff's sale was the most important thing. Without it the whole scheme falls apart."

"So where's the sheriff? I want to arrest him and pitch him in his own jail," a man called out from near Spur.

"We're wondering the same thing. One more point. The law also states that before any sale to recover taxes can be made, the delinquent property owners must all be listed in a notice published in the official county newspaper. That's why the conspirators in this case burned down the *Clarion* three weeks ago so the notices couldn't appear."

The telegraph operator came pushing through the crowd and handed Spur an envelope. He opened it and read it then held it up.

"Help is coming. Listen to this. I wired the Attorney General, the top cop in the state. Listen to this: TO SPUR MCCOY, PINE GROVE, ARIZONA. UNDERSTAND YOUR PROBLEM. SENDING MAN TO RUN SHERIFF'S OFFICE ON MORNING STAGE. ARRIVE TOMORROW AFTERNOON. AVOID ANY MOB ACTION. THE LAW WILL PROTECT THE PEOPLE OF PINE GROVE. HARTLEY WESTOVER, ARIZONA TERRITORIAL ATTORNEY GENERAL."

"So let's find the sheriff so he don't get out of town," somebody yelled.

"Spread out, everyone, and search for the no-good. Don't let him get away."

"Remember, no violence," Spur shouted. "If you find him, bring him back here or to the jail."

The crowd broke up. Some moved down the street looking in the saloons. Some went to the sheriff's house. The livery stable man said he wouldn't rent the sheriff a horse or a rig.

"What about Benscoter?" Gypsy asked. "I've a notion that he's the main conspirator behind all this. Let's not let him get away."

"I doubt if he'll be running," Spur said. "He's got too much invested in this town. Let's go pay him a friendly social call."

They went up the steps and knocked on the door to Benscoter's office, then went inside. His secretary looked up from her desk and smiled.

"Miss Pinnick, how nice to see you," she said.

"Is Mr. Benscoter here?" Spur asked.

"Fact is he stepped out about half an hour ago. Told me he had some things to do and would be gone the rest of the afternoon. He didn't mention any specifics. May I help you?"

"No, we need to see him. Any chance that he went home?"

"I doubt it. He's seldom there except at night. Do you wish to leave a message?"

"No, I don't think so," Gypsy said.

Spur stepped forward quickly and opened the door marked private where he had met with Benscoter before.

"See here!" the secretary said.

Spur pulled the door fully open and looked inside. No one was there.

"Just checking," Spur said. Then he and Gypsy went outside.

"Where does he live?" Spur asked.

Gypsy pointed the way. The street was alive with people chattering about the big scandal. Several men still carried shotguns and rifles. Spur heard that two teams of men had left for the north and south roads out of town to prevent the sheriff from escaping that way.

He'd be found sooner or later. Spur wasn't sure what would happen to the sheriff if the crowd turned ugly again. Down two blocks and over one, they found the Benscoter home. It was the biggest house on the block, three stories of wood and glass, well-painted with lush landscaping around it.

Gypsy lifted a heavy brass knocker on the front door and let it fall. They waited a reasonable time, and Spur dropped the knocker three more times. At last someone opened the door.

"Oh, Mrs. Hartung," Gypsy said, "is Mr. Benscoter at home."

"No, ma'am, just me doing my Friday cleaning. Nobody here. Haven't seen him since morning. She went out about noon someplace."

"Thanks, Mrs. Hartung."

They walked slowly back to Main Street.

"So where is he?" Gypsy asked.

"I'd say hiding somewhere he feels safe. He must have heard and seen what's going on. He knows the secret is out. Not a chance in hell they can have the sheriff's sale now. The whole thing has blown up in his face."

"From that one registered letter you saw?"

"That was part of it. There were too many loose ends he couldn't tie up. He tried hard, had two men killed and still couldn't cover it all."

"It's almost two-thirty," Gypsy said. "Still an hour and a half to the time set for the sheriff's sale. I won't feel that this is all over until that time is past."

"Or we catch the sheriff and throw him in his own jail."

"We can do that?"

"Just watch us. Let's go down to the sheriff's office. I'm taking over as the highest ranking, legally constituted, law officer in the area not under suspicion. I can do that. Had to once or twice. Usually there isn't trouble. How many deputies work with the sheriff?"

"Three, and none of them strong-willed men."

"Good."

They walked in the door of the sheriff's office and found three townsmen there with drawn revolvers.

"Oh, it's you, McCoy," the tallest of the men said. "We're just kind of keeping the peace here and waiting for the sheriff to show up."

"I'll take over here. You three get outside and look for the sheriff."

They nodded, holstered their weapons and went out the door.

"Who's the top deputy here?" Spur demanded. One man came forward. He didn't have a weapon on his hip. Spur looked at the rifle rack and saw that it had been emptied.

"Deputy Higgins, Marshal."

"I'm not a marshal, Higgins. I'm with the Secret Service. You three men know anything about what the sheriff seems to be up to?"

"No sir. Don't know, and nobody will tell us."

Spur filled them in quickly. "What the sheriff has agreed to do is illegal and can get him into a territorial prison for ten to twenty years. He's guilty of conspiracy to defraud if nothing else. If he had anything to do with the two dead men, he's in worse trouble yet. My name is Spur McCoy.

I'm taking over this office until a man gets here tomorrow from the Territorial Attorney General's office. You three understand?"

"Yes sir," all three said.

"Fine. If Sheriff Willard shows up here anytime day or night, he's to be detained, arrested, handcuffed and then put in a cell. Then notify me at once. I'll either be on the street or at my hotel room. We have two men we're hunting, and nobody has the slightest idea how to find them."

"I know how to find at least one of them," someone said from behind Spur. He turned around and saw Flo Benscoter standing in the door of the sheriff's office, smoking a long thin cigar and smiling.

Chapter Thirteen

Spur McCoy looked at Flo Benscoter and chuckled. "You know where to find your husband?"

"I've been married to him for five years. I know most of his small quirks and habits."

"So, Mrs. Benscoter, where is he?" Gypsy asked.

"He went rushing past me on the street a block from his office about half an hour before the big meeting at the courthouse. He figured you'd found him out. He had his hat on with the earflaps. Whenever he puts that on I know he's going up to the cabin. He likes to ski and fish up there. Bought some of those weird long slats and goes sliding down the mountain."

"Can you take us to the cabin, Mrs. Benscoter?" Spur asked.

"I could, if I wanted to." She looked at Spur, her face drawn now, no humor left in it. "Is it true what

I think he planned on doing, the sheriff's sale?"

"We think he was the brains behind it, Mrs. Benscoter," Spur said. "The sheriff isn't smart enough to plan something like this, and Loophole Larson doesn't have the nerve to do it by himself. The postmaster was just a pawn. that leaves J. Lawton as the best candidate."

"What happens to him if I take you up there?"

"Depends on him. If he tries to run again or shoot it out, he'll get hurt. If he surrenders, he'll go to prison for a long, long time."

"Maybe. Your case is a little weak. Two of the conspirators are dead. The only witness you have is the sheriff, if he decides to testify. If he won't talk, you have no case. Or if he gets hung by that mob out there, you also won't have a witness. Chances are looking better and better that J. Lawton could go scot-free in the end. So I'll take you up to the cabin. That way you might not be here when they find Sheriff Willard, and there might be a necktie party before we get back."

Twenty minutes later, Flo had changed into riding pants, boots and a rough jacket, and she and Spur were about to step into saddles.

"I still want to go along," Gypsy said.

"You have a job here, an important one. If you spot the sheriff, you tell him exactly what I told you. Make sure that nobody shoots him or hangs him. He's had a small part in this swindle so far. Tell him we'll guarantee him total immunity from prosecution if he'll testify for the prosecution."

Gypsy nodded and took the .38 revolver out of her reticule. She checked the loads, put it back and waved as the two riders moved west down

Main Street. They didn't take the north or the south road, but headed into the rugged mountains directly west of town. Sharp spires and purple peaks in the distance outlined some of the highest mountains in Arizona.

"Is there really a cabin up here, or is this just a ploy to get me out of town?"

"Oh, there's a cabin all right, and my best bet is that J. Lawton is there, probably with that *puta* he's been fucking, that little slut Clarissa from the whorehouse. Sure, I know all about her. She isn't half the woman I am, and she gets paid for it."

"Then why are you leading me up there?"

"J. Lawton has done some mean things in his time, but cheating these people out of their property and most of their life's savings is too much. Besides, I want to see him squirm when I catch him with that bitch."

"Love conquers all," Spur said.

"True love, not fucking love," Flo said. "Besides, maybe we could tie him up and make him watch me seduce you and then fuck your brains right through your skull. I'd enjoy that. It would make him go crazy wild."

"You could live with him doing twenty years in the territorial prison in Yuma?"

"Easy. He's still the richest man in town, and the court would give me control of everything he owns. I've got lawyers, too."

"That would make him even unhappier, wouldn't it?"

"Knowing that I was spending his money while he was in prison would drive him insane and he'd never last six months in jail." She snorted. "Do I look stupid to you?"

It took them nearly an hour to get to the cabin, about four miles up some rough trail that degenerated into a single line track up a narrow canyon.

"He skis down there in winter. Sometimes I thought he'd break his neck. He used to bring me up here before we got married. Now he brings his sluts."

They came around a small bend in the trail and could see the log cabin 100 yards ahead. She stopped and held up her hand. Smoke came from the chimney, and two horses stood at the tie rail at the side.

"Damned if I wasn't right. He knew the situation had gotten out of hand. If the sale went through, he'd be in clover. If it didn't, nobody would think to look for him up here."

Flo slid off her horse and ground tied it. "We walk from here through the woods so he can't see us coming, not that he'd be looking. He's still probably humping that little whore of his. Damn, I hate that slut."

They came up to the side of the cabin that didn't have any windows. Spur ordered Flo to stay back, and he edged around the corner, ducked under a window and made it to the door. He grabbed the knob and turned it. Not locked. He eased the panel open half an inch. No squeak. He peered through and saw a stove, a table and three chairs.

Another inch crack and he spotted the bed. Two naked forms lay there, pumping up and down, low moans and squeals coming from the pair.

Spur pushed open the door and stepped inside, his boots hitting the wooden floor. J. Lawton, on top, looked at Spur and bellowed in anger.

"What the hell are you doing up here?" He scrambled off the girl and toward a shotgun that leaned against the wall near the head of the bed. Spur put a round into the weapon's wooden stock, blasting it off the wall and skidding it six feet away down the side wall.

"Bastard!"

The girl sat up on the bed, not trying to cover herself.

Flo ran in through the front door, a six-gun in her hand.

"Well, well, look at the lovers. Isn't this just too damn sweet for words? True love, at last you've found it, Jethro, up here in the woods with your fucking little slut."

"Flo, you brought him?" Disbelief pulsed through the words as J. Lawton looked at his wife with anger and shock.

"Get your pants on, lover. You're going down to town to stand trial for conspiracy, for bribing a postal employee, for extortion, for trying to swindle the good folks out of their property, and, oh yes, for the murder of Jessie and Loophole."

"You out of your mind, Flo?"

"Won't take much to dig up the scum you hired to ride Jessie out of town and kill him. Probably at the Blue Goose right now. As for Loophole, that was stupid. That barkeep will see the light and admit he never did see Loophole in the bar or behind it until somebody found his shot-up body. Hell, Jethro Lawton Benscoter, you're gonna hang so high it won't be worth missing. People will come from miles around just to see your feet twitch and your tongue stick out and your eyes bulge as your neck snaps."

J. Lawton stood there, clenching and unclenching his hands. At last he let them drop to his sides.

"The lady is right, Benscoter. You better get your britches on and dress for a ride. You'll be in jail tonight."

Flo walked closer, still holding the Colt. "Jethro Lawton, you'll be in jail tonight or in hell. You call it. Which one do you want?"

"Put down the gun, Flo," Spur said. He was too far away to do much about her weapon, and he certainly didn't want to shoot her.

"Call it, Jethro Lawton. You want me to kill you or just shoot you up a little? You remember I was with a Wild West show as a pistol shot before you married me."

His eyes went wide, one hand coming up to cover his heart. He reached out with his other hand.

"Flo, you wouldn't do this. You can't do this."

"The hell I won't. Jail or hell, you bastard?"

"Jail," he said, so softly that Spur barely heard him. Spur lunged toward her, but Flo fired the .38 revolver twice. Both rounds found their mark. One smashed into Benscoter's right knee and one into his left knee. He screamed in agony and hatred and fury as he crumpled to the floor, naked and now bleeding from his smashed knees.

"Oh, God!" Spur said.

Flo flipped the weapon over in the air, caught it by the barrel and handed it to Spur.

"Come on, whore, get your clothes on. The party and the pay days for you are over. Jethro Lawton, I guess the least I can do is help you get dressed. I'll let the federal lawman here bind up your knees so you don't bleed to death. There must be some old sheets around here he can use for bandages."

Two hours later they rode into a wildly celebrating Pine Grove. There were lanterns strung across the street. A wide swatch across it had been swept down to the hardpan. An impromptu orchestra beat out a dance tempo, and two dozen dancers kicked up their heels across the dirt floor.

Spur and the three others rode down to the jail. Flo found Doc Johnson and had him go to the jail, then she went to her house to relax in a hot bubble bath.

At the jail, Spur found one deputy holding down the place with Gypsy beating him at a game of poker with matches for chips.

She bounced up, long black hair flying, her dark eyes checking on Spur who came carrying Benscoter over his back. She guided Spur into a cell and only then saw the bloody bandages on both of Benscoter's knees.

Without saying a word, Spur let Benscoter down on the bunk and stepped out of the cell, then closed it and locked the door.

"Doc will be over soon," he said and walked back into the main office.

"So tell me!" Gypsy said, grabbing at his sleeve.

Spur took a cup of coffee from the pot on the small stove and drank it half down, then he recounted the uneventful capture.

"She actually shot him in both knees?"

"From about ten feet and so fast I'd swear it was one long sound in that cabin. Maybe she did used to be a Wild West show gun shooter."

"Would she have killed him if he told her he wanted to go straight to hell?"

"I thought so at the time, but on the way back she confided that she wouldn't have done that. I'd have had to arrest her for murder, and then she wouldn't get to enjoy all of Benscoter's money. She said she figured he might be able to beat the conspiracy charges and the fraud charges, if the sheriff got killed as he was captured or if he refused to testify against Benscoter But she said she figured he would be convicted of the murders of Loophole and Jessie. He had the motive and the opportunity with Loophole, and she's sure he hired someone to shoot down Jessie."

"So the chances are high that Benscoter will hang and she will inherit his fortune, which must be considerable even without what he was trying to steal," Gypsy said.

"Right. Now all we have to do is find the sheriff and we can wrap this up. Why the big celebration? I figured somebody must have captured the lawman and had him in jail."

"Nope, not yet. They decided that since the sheriff didn't show up for the sale at four o'clock, he'd lost and they wanted a celebration. They got it started about five, and there's more whiskey and barrels of beer and cornjack out there than I've seen in years. Two bunches of musicians are going to play all night just as long as anyone wants to dance."

Doc Johnson came through the door, and Spur took him to the cell.

"Afraid we have a nasty pair of wounds, Doc. Benscoter got himself nailed in both knees by a sharpshooter—not me. See if you can fix him up well enough so he can walk to his own trap door on the scaffold complete with a hangman's noose."

Doc Johnson took off the makeshift bandages and shook his head. "Somebody did a hell of a job on these knees. Not one chance in ten that he'll be able to walk in six months, let alone in a month when the gallows will be ready."

Spur talked with the deputy in charge, warning him that if Benscoter got out of jail the deputy would hang in his place.

Spur and Gypsy walked up Main to the celebration and took a quick two-step whirl around the street. They visited the punch bowl and found it was cider generously laced with whiskey. After a sip, Gypsy put her cup down.

They sat in chairs brought out from many of the stores and watched the dancers.

"What's the chances of finding the sheriff?" Gypsy asked.

"Not too good. Come night he can slip out of town fifteen dozen places and be halfway to Phoenix by morning. With a good horse and a clear night, he'd make good time."

"Oh, the lawman coming from Phoenix sent a wire to the mayor. He said he was bringing two additional men with him to insure they could maintain law and order in Pine Grove. All three will be here tomorrow afternoon on the regular stage run."

"More the better. Want to dance?" he asked.

"Not really. You want to come to my place for a nice quiet piece of cherry pie?"

"With whipped cream?"

"Out of whipped cream, but you can have two pieces of pie."

"Done."

A short time later in Gypsy's house, Spur stretched out in an overstuffed chair, put his feet on an ottoman and took a second bite of the best cherry pie he'd had in months. Cherry pie was one of his failings. He'd die for a fine cherry pie.

"You like it?" Gypsy asked.

"Good enough to eat," Spur said, using a line he'd learned years ago, but it still got a laugh now and then. Gypsy laughed. She had a piece herself, and when she finished it, she carried her dish and fork back to the kitchen and returned with a second slice of pie for Spur.

"I was just joking about another pie," Spur said.

"You were not. Cherry pie is your favorite."

"How did you know?"

She smiled. "You told me in a weak moment."

He ate the second piece. They talked about the hunt for the sheriff, which would continue in the morning outside of town. Somebody must have seen him. It didn't matter a lot if they caught him or not. No real damage was done on the sheriff's sale that didn't happen, and they had plenty of evidence to convict Benscoter of murder. Spur would get going on that first thing in the morning.

"Let's sit in the porch swing," Gypsy said.

"You like that swing."

"I had my first real kiss out there when I was sixteen."

"Lead the way."

He let her sit down first and pushed her a while.

"I can see the moon through the trees," she said. "Come and take a look."

He sat beside her and kept the swing moving with his feet on the porch floor. It was dark out, but they were splotched with the moonlight coming through the trees.

"Why do people think the moon is romantic?" Gypsy asked, turning toward him.

"Not sure, but a guess would be that a lot of romantic things like first kisses take place at night in the dark under a moon somewhere.

Moonlight means darkness, and a lot of people do things in the dark they wouldn't try in the daylight."

"Good explanation. I'll remember that." She moved closer to him. "Remember how I told you how I felt when you kissed me so long the other day?"

"I remember."

"Did it make you feel all kind of warm and cozy and wanting things, too?"

"Lady, you're getting on dangerous ground here."

"I know, but it's dark, and people try things." She moved over and kissed him. Her mouth came open and her tongue teased his lips until they opened. She sighed and melted against him, her breasts pressing hard on his chest.

He came away from her lips.

"Don't stop," she said and kissed him again. Her hand strayed down to his leg and lay there on his thigh, not moving, just making contact.

He eased his lips from hers. She caught his hand and put it over one of her breasts.

"Gypsy."

"Hush, it's dark. Who's to know. Please, pet me. Make me feel like you want me. It's important to me right now."

She kissed him again before he could reply. Her mouth was open and her tongue darted into his mouth.

He eased away. "Gypsy, this is not what I should be doing."

"Spur, don't talk. I'll tell you if I have to. I'm not a virgin, Spur McCoy, and I bet you aren't either. You're not stealing something from me. I've made love before, and I swore I'd be sure I wanted to the next time. Right now is the next time. Spur McCoy, I want to show you my gratitude and my thanks for finding out what happened at the newspaper and to my father. Let me do that for you."

Chapter Fourteen

Spur's hand seemed to have a mind of its own. Gently it caressed her soft breast, and she nodded.

"Oh, yes! That feels so fine. Kiss me again and keep doing that. Oh, yes!"

He kissed her, leaving room for his hand to work. He could feel her nipple harden under her dress. He found a button and undid it, then a second one, and his hand crept inside her dress.

He touched something silky, a chemise. It was loose. He pulled it up, and then his hand crept upward and touched the edge of a breast.

Gypsy trembled. Her tongue darted deeper into his mouth, then she sighed again and her lips left his. "Darling Spur, you don't know how long I've wanted you to touch me, to pet me that way. Yes, yes. Don't ever stop. Oh, great lord, that is so fine."

His tweaked at her nipple, and she pushed her hips against him. He caught her hand and moved it over so it covered the growing bulge under his pants. Her eyes widened in the dappled moonlight, and then she smiled and snuggled against his hand under her dress.

He stroked and caressed both breasts and kissed her again.

"Gypsy, it might be better if we went inside."

"Oh, yes!"

She stood at once, caught his hand, hurried him through the screen door and led him to her bed-room.

He let go of her hand and lit the lamp there. She ran out and brought back two more lit lamps and put one on the dresser and one on a nightstand beside the bed. She grinned.

"I want to see everything," she said. Gypsy checked to make sure the blind was drawn tightly over the bedroom window, then she came back to him and hugged him so her entire body pressed hard against his. Her lips found his and she kissed him with that light feathery touch, then let go of him and lay on the bed.

He stretched out beside her. They were both still fully clothed, only the two buttons open on her dress. He took her hand and put it on the erection bulging his pants.

"Open the buttons," he said.

She nodded and undid his belt buckle, then the buttons on his fly. Her hand slid inside his pants over his underwear, and she gasped when she felt his erection.

He kissed her again, held her tight and whispered, "Do you want both of us to take off our clothes?"

"Just you first," she said, grinning.

He pulled off his boots, then slid out of his pants and removed his vest and then his town shirt. He wore no undershirt.

She sat up and touched his chest, running her hand over the hairy surfaces, brushing his nipples, smiling and running her hand down the hairy patch that led inside his underwear at his waist.

He touched her dress. She nodded and sat up and pulled it off over her head. She left the chemise in place, hiding her breasts. She wore some of the newer bloomers, loose, halfway to the knee. A strip of bare flesh showed between her bloomers and the bottom of her chemise. He ran his hand under the silky cloth and caught one breast.

She gasped, then nodded, and his other hand captured a breast. She touched the bulge in his short underwear.

"Oh, my!" she whispered. "I've never felt this way before, like I wanted to stay here the rest of my life. Like nothing is important but what we're doing right now. Like I'll love you forever and ever no matter what happens."

His hands left her breast, and gently he lifted the chemise up to her chin. She nodded, and he lofted it over her head and trailed it down her back until it came free of her waist-length black hair.

Her breasts showed with pink areolas, brighter now with sexual arousal, her nipples a deeper red and erect, pulsing when he touched them.

Spur bent and kissed the swell of one breast, and she gasped. He kissed it again and again as he fondled the other with his hand. He licked her breast and then nibbled at her nipple with his teeth.

Gypsy gasped and her eyes went wide, then she grabbed him and fell on top of him on the bed.

Her breath came in small gasps and her hips pounded against his, then her whole body shook and vibrated as a spasm shot through her, exciting every nerve ending. She moaned low and soft, then louder until it rose to a keening wail as she jolted against him another dozen times as the spasms rolled through her again and again and again.

Spur held her tightly, one hand still on a breast. She gave one last moan and lay still, her breath coming in a long series of gulps and gasps. At last she lay quietly on top of him. She opened one eye and stared down at him, then pushed back so she could focus on his face.

"Nothing like that has ever happened to me before. What a wonder you are! You kissed my titties and I went wild." She bent and brushed her lips across his cheek. "Miracle man, you truly are a miracle worker."

She sat up and urged him up, then pulled down on his short underwear. He lifted his hips off the bed and she tugged the cloth down until it slipped over his penis which swung upward, stiff and ready.

"Oh my!" Her eyes went wide, and she looked at him. "He's so . . . so huge!" Gypsy's hand moved toward it, then stopped.

"I like to be touched, too," he said. She smiled then and brushed the shaft with her hand, then held him and gripped him tightly for a moment.

"Oh, so big."

He kissed her lips lightly. "Don't worry. We'll fit together. You'll have lots of room."

She looked up at him, her face edged with worry, then a slow smile broke through. "Of course. Women have babies and they come right out through—" She stopped and giggled. "Through the same place."

She pulled the underwear off his feet, then lay down again and pulled him on top of her.

"Just lay there a minute. This is all happening so fast. A girl dreams of this for years, and then when it happens, she needs to slow down a little and think about it and wonder and feel how good it all is." She smiled up at him.

"It's just as good as I dreamed. I told you I wasn't a virgin. That first time was when I was seventeen and the boy was sixteen and we didn't know what we were doing. He tried, but I'm not sure he ever actually got inside of me. He made a mess of sticky stuff all over my legs and then he yelled and grinned and got up and ran away."

"I won't run away. Promise."

She looked at him, and the delight turned her face into one of total beauty. She kissed him hard on the lips. "Make me naked like you are," she said.

She helped him take down her bloomers. Her hips had a little more womanly flair than he had guessed, and her swatch of black pubic hair made a rectangle up from her crotch more than a V. She looked down at her naked body and lifted her brows.

"Now you know. This is all of me, naked and ready for whatever you want."

He kissed her, warming her breasts as he did, then one hand moved down to her crotch and she trembled. He worked up both inner thighs, then eased one leg away from the other. She looked at him, then pulled his face to her and kissed him. As the kiss lasted he brushed his fingers across her heartland.

He felt the moist outer lips, and she jolted when he touched them. Her mouth left his.

"Oh, lordy, do that again!"

He brushed them, then again, and each time she responded. Gently he found her hard node and stroked it back and forth.

She looked at him curiously. "Oh, my!" He stroked her clit again and again, and she yelped in total delight. Her hips began moving against him and then she wailed and kicked into a furious climax that shook her body. It was over quickly, and she frowned and looked at him.

"That's a little trigger down there that sets you off in a hurry," he said.

"There's so much to find out, to learn about." She sat up. "Let me look at you. I've never really looked down there before."

She explored him, fingered his heavy scrotum and stared in wonder again at his long tool.

"It just gets hard this way when you get excited?"

"Yes. Otherwise it would be tough walking around."

"Not fair. Women's breasts are big all the time."

"But they get bigger when they fill with milk for a baby. Haven't you noticed with mothers?"

"I guess. I've never thought about it."

She lay down and pulled him over her. "You really think it'll fit?"

"I think so."

He massaged her outer lips and stroked one finger deep inside her slot. She yelped when he did it, but he brought out her juices and wet her more.

He spread her legs, knelt between them and lifted her knees. Her eyes sparkled as she watched him.

"Soon?"

He nodded, bent and placed himself against her lips and eased forward. For a moment there was resistance, then he edged in a little and the expression on her face blossomed into rapture.

He edged in more and more, and her juices welcomed him. In an instant he sank in until their pelvic bones nudged together and he could penetrate no farther.

"Oh, I'm gonna melt!" Gypsy whispered. "That's just the most wonderful thing—ever!"

Slowly he began to ease out and stroke back in. Her face beamed then her hips picked up the motion and worked upward to meet his downward strokes.

"Oh, yes," she whispered. "How can people say this can be wrong when it feels so wonderful?"

With each stroke he brushed across her clit, and after a dozen ministrations she burst into another climax, shaking and jolting and wailing like the end of the world had come. He kept stroking as she tapered off.

Sweat beaded her forehead. She still panted like a small steam engine, and her smile was magnificent. She closed her eyes and rested a moment, then her hips worked again and she looked up at him.

"Isn't it your turn? Don't you do something, too?"

Spur grinned. "Yes, but it takes me a little longer."

"Can I help?"

"You are." He drove in harder and faster then. He felt her knees around his sides as she lifted them higher. He slipped in deeper and increased his speed. The pressure built slowly, then higher and higher. He knew the juices were coming, the gates opening, the dam about to burst.

Spur grunted and panted and whispered again. "Oh, yes, yes, yes." Then the whole world exploded, and he came again and again in great spurts.

As his body stopped shaking, he realized Gypsy had climaxed again as well. She eased down from her ecstasy, and her eyes opened. She smiled. He'd never seen a more wonderful, happy, contented smile in his life.

They both eased down from their peaks holding each other tightly, then trying to relax and bring their breathing back to normal.

After a time, she touched his face and he opened his eyes and looked at her.

"Spur McCoy, this is so marvelous, so beautiful, just so, so wonderful, why do adults ever do anything else but make love?"

"That's a question I never can find an answer to. Maybe it's because people have to eat, and that takes work and forces the man and woman apart to get the work done to obtain the food. The problem is the more they make love, the more babies they have and the more food they need, so it takes more work."

She giggled. "I guess that makes as much sense as anything." She pulled his face down and kissed him, long and soft and possessively.

"Now, Spur McCoy, you're here and it's dark out and I don't want you to risk going back to the old hotel, so you have to stay here with me all night."

"You sure? What will the neighbors think?"

"I don't care. Anyway, you can leave just as it gets light before any of them get up." She kissed him. "You know that I love you, Spur McCoy? I know it's a just-getting-fucked kind of love, but I love you."

"You said the bad word."

"It seemed right. I've said it before, when I was alone, practicing so I'd be able to say it when I needed it."

"Shameless."

"You made me that way. I've often wondered how I'd feel after my first real lovemaking. It's nothing like I figured. I don't feel all that different. More like I have learned something, experienced something that I'll understand and use the rest of my life. But it didn't make a different person or anything like that."

"You thought it might?"

"A girl never knows. I've been dreaming about this since I was thirteen. That's a third of my life."

"Oh." He lay there with her head on his chest, his hands laced behind his head. He usually put his hands back there when he was waiting for a woman or after he'd made love. He wondered why.

"Can I ask a question?" he said.

"Yes, anything."

"Do you have any more of that wonderful cherry pie?"

"Only if you'll stay all night and make love to me again and again until we're exhausted."

He frowned. "How about a fresh pot of coffee to keep up our strength?"

"You got it," Gypsy said. She crawled over him, her long black hair trailing behind her as she scampered, naked, for the kitchen. Spur McCoy ran lightly after her, feeling like a kid of 18 again. He gloried in the feeling. Too soon morning would come and with it the harsher realities of finding the sheriff.

"Hey, where are you, McCoy?" Gypsy called.

Spur hurried into the kitchen.

Chapter Fifteen

Spur McCoy opened up the Home Café the next morning at six A.M. He had coffee, a high stack of flapjacks, three eggs and six slices of bacon. Then he went to the courthouse and checked with the deputy sheriff on duty, the youngest of the three who had drawn night duty.

Benscoter still lay in his cell, bellowing and complaining. He shut up as soon as he saw Spur.

"Benscoter, you going to take this prosecution all alone, or do you know where ex-sheriff Willard might be hiding?"

"Bastard ran out on me."

"You ran out on him first, didn't you? You high-tailed it up to your cabin."

"Yeah, so sue me. Throw me in jail. You can't hurt me any more than you have, damn you!"

"Now that you've got that out of your craw, do you know where Willard is so we can put him in a cell beside you?"

"Hell, yes. He's got a place two miles north on the road to Flag, but it's a damn fortress. He's got all sorts of weapons up there and traps and pits and a dozen ways to keep a whole posse off his land."

"Two miles north. Which side of the road?"

"To the right, up a skinny little canyon that ends at a sheer cliff nobody can climb up or down lessen you want to dangle on a rope for two hundred feet."

"He alone?"

"Think he took Ruth with him. She's one of the girls at the saloon he likes. Nice looking little whore."

"Might just pay him a visit. How are the knees?"

"Hurt like hell."

"Good, you deserve it."

"I want to see my lawyer."

"You don't have one. You shot him, remember?"

"The other lawyer. I'll pay him good."

"Guess that's your right. I'll tell the deputy."

An hour later, Spur left on a horse from the livery. He had the repeating rifle again, with a box of shells, a rope, five sticks of dynamite all capped and with 15-second burning fuses.

He rode out for what he judged was two miles and found only a flat gentle valley as he worked along the ridges and slopes toward Flagstaff. He kept moving. A half mile beyond, he discovered a valley to the right that quickly rose and turned into a narrow canyon that ended in a sheer rock wall maybe a half mile away.

He slid off his mount and checked his gear. He put the rifle around his back on its sling, adjusted his .45 Colt in leather and checked the extra box of rounds for the .45. He had the rifle rounds loose in his jacket pocket and eight in the weapon ready to fire. He tied the lariat rope to his belt at his side. Time to go.

Spur worked along an easy trail for 300 yards, then felt it was time to leave the track. He angled 20 yards into the woods so he could still see the trail and parallel it, watching for tree falls, pits, tied back saplings or young trees, anything that could be a lethal trap for the unwary. He found nothing like that along this stretch.

He took his time. He had all day. He had all week. No reason to rush except he didn't bring any food with him. There would be food in the cabin.

After he had worked another 200 yards forward, he moved cautiously back to the trail. From there he could see a cabin, maybe a quarter of a mile ahead. No smoke came from the chimney. This could be an exercise in futility.

He stayed closer to the trail this time and moved forward. It was early. Maybe the sheriff was still asleep. Spur was no more than ten yards from the trail now, and directly ahead he saw a small pine tree bent back. He stopped and examined the ground in front of it.

Spur picked up the trigger at once—a piece of twine stretched from a small stake in the ground to another stake where it wasn't tied, only positioned around. The first time an animal or a man kicked that twine, it would release the tied back tree and some lethal device would be slammed forward with great force and impale or crush the victim. He didn't look to see what the weapon was.

Spur found a half dozen rocks and threw them one at a time at the trigger twine. The fifth one hit the string and drove it forward.

The result was quick. The pine tree rammed forward with a swishing of the air and a six-inch thick log three feet long slammed forward with it chest high. The log would have crushed anyone's ribs into their chest.

Spur went around the trap, faded another ten yards into the brush and woods and worked forward. Had these traps been here all the time, or had Willard recently set them up?

It took Spur ten minutes more to work his way to within 50 yards of the small log cabin. Now a stream of smoke came from the chimney and Spur nodded. Someone was inside. All he had to do was find out who it was. If it was Willard he'd arrest him and take him back to jail in Pine Grove—if he was lucky. It depended on how desperate the sheriff was.

Spur lay in the brush looking past a small pine tree at the cabin for ten more minutes. It was a recon, judging the target, figuring how to take it, what risks were involved, how best to attack the problem, trying to find any weakness.

Plug up the chimney and make the stove smoke was always good, but he had no available material to use on the chimney. Pine boughs might work, but if the fire was hot they would simply burn away and the smoke would escape normally. Besides, there was no good access to the roof.

He wondered what areas would be set with traps. He moved so he could see the rear of the cabin. There was a second door with two horses tied there. Willard wouldn't risk any traps around the horses. First Spur would take the horses and hide them. There was no window in the back, so he should be able to get away with the horses.

He moved cautiously to the edge of the timber, but saw no places where the leaves or needles of the forest floor had been disturbed. He found a dead branch four feet long and jammed it into the ground in front of him as he walked. He was within 20 feet of the rear door when the stick suddenly sank into the ground right in front of his foot. He drew the stick out and looked. A thin lattice work of branches held up some netting that had been covered carefully with leaves and twigs and pine needles to make it look natural. He probed to the side and found it went about four feet wide.

Cautiously he worked his way around the pit, then headed again for the horses. He spoke quietly to them as he came up to them. At once he saw the bells attached to the mounts' bridles. Ordinary head movement did not ring the bells, but a sustained walk or gallop would make them ring.

Spur cut the leather leads that held the bells on the mounts and checked them again. Nothing else. He caught the reins of both animals and with his probe, followed the hoofprints the animals used to walk into the area.

Five minutes later he had the horses hidden 50 yards from the cabin. He went back and stared at the place again. Two sticks of dynamite wedged tightly at the bottom of the door should blow the panel inward. He could be just around the corner of the cabin and rush around and cover the stunned sheriff inside.

Before he placed the dynamite he went over his route with his probe. He found no pits dug, but there was a small pine tree bent back and tied. It took him five minutes to find the trigger. The weapon was a two inch thick pole, two feet long, that had 30 or 40 sharpened sticks protruding from it at many angles. The sticks were strong enough to kill a man if it struck him anywhere in the belly, chest or head.

Cautiously, Spur cut the leather thongs that held the deadly spiked log. He cut three of the thongs and then held the log by one end and lowered it to the ground. Now tripping the twine would do nothing but release the tree to swing forward.

His route was clear. Spur set the two sticks of dynamite and pushed the end of one of them into a crack under the door. He wedged the second beside it, then lit one of the 15-second fuses with a match and hurried around the corner of the cabin.

One fuse would set off the dynamite cap pushed into the one stick of powder which would set off the other one instantaneously.

The fuse burned for 20 seconds, then a cracking roar ripped through the peaceful quiet of the morning. With the explosion, Spur raced around the corner of the cabin, his .45 out. Smoke still hovered over the whole door opening.

Spur heard a six-gun fire and sensed the round blast through the smoky doorway. He ducked low, pushed through the smoke and tried to see something. The small cabin had filled with the vapors from the explosion.

It blew out both front windows as well, and a breeze soon thinned out the smoke so he could see.

Sheriff Ben Willard lay on the floor near a bunk on the far side of the cabin. He had the six-gun in his hand but it sagged toward the floor. His leg stuck out at an odd angle. Broken, Spur decided.

A woman got up from the bunk. She held her head and stared around as if not sure where she was.

Spur advanced on the sheriff slowly. He worked around a broken table, past a tumbled chair and a splintered half of the door.

The sheriff didn't move. He was fully dressed. Breakfast was cooking on the small wood burning stove to the far side. The sheriff's pants leg was red with blood. The six-gun fell from his hand and the force of the fall dropped the hammer on a live round. The firing made a thunderous sound in the small enclosed cabin as the bullet thudded into the wall.

Spur jumped over to the man and covered him with his .45. Sheriff Willard didn't move. He looked down at his right leg through glinting eyes.

"My damn leg. Part of the door, I think."

Slowly and with care, Spur eased up the lawman's right pants leg. Then he saw higher up where a giant splinter from the door had ripped through the heavy part of the lower leg.

Blood gushed from the wound. Spur hurried to the small kitchen and found two dishtowels. He tore them into strips, came back and bound them around the wound—leg, splinter and all.

"Better get you to a doctor soon as we can," Spur said.

Ben Willard's color was better though he'd lost a lot of blood. He rubbed one hand over his face. "You know about the sheriff's sale due for yesterday?"

"It all came out. We've got Benscoter in jail. You'll get a cell beside his. You're just as guilty as he is."

"How much time will I get?"

"I'd say two years. Depends on the judge. Also depends if you testify for the prosecution."

"I'll testify if I don't get charged with the crime."

"I can't do that. Talk to the District Attorney when we get back. Maybe you can work out something."

Spur picked up the gun from the floor. "You have any more weapons in the cabin?"

"No, just that one."

"I'm going to go get the horses. If you try to keep me out when I get back, I'll ride for town and let you rot up here. By morning that leg will drive you insane."

"Won't try nothing. Get the horses. Oh, watch them pits. Got a few of them. Follow the hoof prints, best way."

Nearly two hours later, Spur arrived at Doc Johnson's office with his prisoner. The whore had not been hurt, only dazed, and she gratefully went back to her saloon.

Doc Johnson took a look and said, "Have him patched up in an hour. Send a deputy over to take him to the jail. He won't be walking. Better bring a wheelbarrow."

When Spur walked into the sheriff's office he found more than a dozen people there. Gypsy had her notebook and pencil and came over and grabbed his hand. She led him to a tall, silver-haired man.

"Spur McCoy, I'd like you to meet Jerico Domero. He's the assistant Attorney General for the territory and has come to take over the county law work until we can elect a new sheriff."

The two shook hands. Spur liked this tall, bronzed man with the white hair. He didn't look over 35.

"Hear you've been doing your share of rounding up the bad guys," Domero said.

"Figured I'd help out a little until you got here. Ex-Sheriff Ben Willard is over at Doc Johnson's office getting a log cut out of his leg. You might want to send a deputy over there to bring him back. Oh, Doc said to bring a wheelbarrow."

Domero nodded, moved away and talked to one of his men.

"Things been happening fast and furious here," Gypsy said. "The stage left Phoenix at three A.M. so it could get here early. Domero has been whipping things into shape fast. He's already charged Benscoter with two counts of murder as well as the sheriff's sale fraud. He said it will be grand larceny and conspiracy."

"Sounds like he has things well in hand."

"Let's leave here. I want to talk to you."

They went out into the soft noontime sunshine and walked in the mountain air.

"You were really terribly wicked last night, Spur McCoy, to lead me on that way until I just let you do anything you wanted to do with me."

Spur chuckled.

"I guess I seduced you, didn't I? I just wanted to make love so much that I couldn't control myself. So I want to thank you."

She squeezed his hand.

"Your thanks are noted and appreciated."

"More thanks will come later in a more personal, intimate fashion. Now, it looks to me like Domero has things well in hand. He'll want to talk to you again, I'm sure, to get more details about what you've done here, but that can wait until tomorrow. Right now I want to take you to dinner, lunch, whatever you call it. My treat, I get to pay. Let's go to the Home Café. Terri is a special friend of mine."

He told her about the capture of Sheriff Willard.

"Domero might let Willard off easy if he can testify or give any eyewitness evidence about Benscoter talking about killing either Jessie or Loophole. We'll see. Now about us."

"Us?" Spur asked.

"Of course. You don't think you can toy with a lady's affections that way, violate her most precious treasure, and simply kiss her on the cheek and walk away."

Spur looked at her sharply, and she giggled. "I figured that would get your attention. What I really want to know is how your wounded arm is. Bet you haven't had it checked since the doc patched you up. Really, McCoy, you need a full-time nurse. I suggest that you wire your superiors in Washington and tell them that this case is wrapped up, but you'll need to stay here two or three days to give testimony and talk with the new law officers. Also you have an arm wound that needs some healing time."

"When I do this, who would I get to be my private nurse to watch over me night and day?"

Gypsy flipped a handful of black hair over her shoulder and smiled at him. It was a smile and a face he would find hard to forget.

"Oh, we might be able to find someone who could do those difficult tasks. Might even find someone who would do them all with no charge to the government, not even for the board and room."

"I can't imagine who."

"Oh, another development. I had a talk with Florence Benscoter. She's in charge now of all of her husband's businesses. She says her husband's feud with Papa was silly. As soon as I get the regular paper going again, she'll want to talk to me about advertising. Which means I'll be in much better financial condition."

"Any more news running around?"

"Well, one little thing. The box social is set for day after tomorrow, and you better be there. I'll tell you what my basket looks like. All the funds will go toward my new building for the *Clarion*. Mrs. Benscoter says she knows that her husband had a hand in how my father died, and she's guaranteed that if we don't raise at least three hundred dollars, she'll make up the balance. She also said the bank would be more than happy to give me a no interest loan to rebuild the *Clarion* office and even get a new press and the printing and paper supplies I'll need. So, looks like some good might come out of all of this after all."

When they had finished their lunch, she stood and headed for the back door that led to the alley, motioning him to follow. In the alley she looked around and saw no one.

"I just had to kiss you right away or I knew that I would explode. Do you mind?"

She put her arms around him and kissed him hard. When she eased away, Spur McCoy smiled.

"Don't mind the kissing at all. Fact is, I kind of like it. About that board and room and nurse care. Does that include any cherry pie?"

Gypsy Pinnick laughed and nodded. "Cherry pie every day is a specialty of the house. That and a wonderfully soft feather bed every morning and evening."

"It works for me," Spur McCoy said and grinned.